Old Belgrave Hall.

In Plain Sight

Based on the True Story of Leicester's Jesuit Martyr

Kate Myers

Matador
9 Priory Business Park,
Wistow Road, Kibworth Beauchamp,
Leicestershire. LE8 0RX
Tel: 0116 279 2299
Email: books@troubador.co.uk
Web: www.troubador.co.uk/matador
Twitter: @matadorbooks

ISBN: 978 1788038 812

British Library Cataloguing in Publication Data.
A catalogue record for this book is available from the British Library.

Printed and bound in the UK by 4edge Limited
Typeset in 11pt Minion Pro by Troubador Publishing Ltd, Leicester, UK

Matador is an imprint of Troubador Publishing Ltd

CONTENTS

Acknowledgments ix

List of Illustrations x

1682   Arrest in Leicester 1

1692   Leicester, Ten years later 4

1641   Leicester Before the Civil War 15

1652   After the Civil War,
       Eleven Years Later 18

1653   Gardening 34

1661   Death, The Uninvited Guest 50

1678   The Popish Plot 67

1681   The Net Tightens 79

1682   Leicester Gaol 99

1683   An Unwelcome Succession 118

1689   Hunted 138

1690   Leicester 157

1692   Quarantine 178

1692   November 184

Afterword 192

Key to the plan of Medieval Leicester 207

ACKNOWLEDGEMENTS

I would like to acknowledge the invaluable help and advice given by Rebecca Somerset, archivist of the British Province of the Society of Jesus, and by Rev. William Myers, Emeritus Professor and editor of Restoration and Revolution (Croom Helm, 1986). My husband's understanding of this period and his support have made this work possible.

I would also like to thank Fr Isidore Clarke OP whose Short History of the Dominicans in Leicester(DeMontfort University, 1997) first acquainted me with Fr William Bentney SJ. I wish to thank the former provincial of the Society of Jesus, the Very Rev. James Crampsey SJ, for coming to Leicester and helping to unveil a Blue Plaque in Fr Bentney's honour, and to the current provincial, Fr Dermot Preston SJ, for agreeing to add his thoughts on this once forgotten priest to the Afterword.

Finally, I wish to express my gratitude to the staff at the Leicestershire Records Office and the University of Leicester library who have been most helpful and to Hugo DeLauncey for his excellent sketch of old Belgrave Hall.

LIST OF ILLUSTRATIONS

Old Belgrave Hall (frontisepiece)

Hindlip Hall

A Diagram of Priest Hides in Harvington Hall

A Plan of Medieval Leicester with Key to the Plan

Stukeleys Map of Leicester 1722

1682

ARREST IN LEICESTER

Mornings usually started with a cock crow, followed by cows moaning to be milked, the smell of ovens fired up baking bread, the gentle clatter of shutters being opened, the swish of curtains drawn back. A village awakening.

Not that morning.

The inhabitants of Belgrave Hall heard the rough shouts of a sargeant barking at his troop of militia, the stomping of heavy feet marching ever closer. A horse and cart trundled along the turnpike road behind them. Peering from upstairs windows, over the garden wall, they could see Leicester's enforcers, burly men, most with muskets, spoiling for action.

This was a time of peace, nearly forty years since the Civil War. There was no den of thieves or brigands about. At a command their destination became all too clear. They forced their way through the gates and in short order surrounded the Hall. They'd come to search the place from top to bottom, out to apprehend a reported Jesuit priest said to be harbouring there.

The Byerley family were known Roman Catholics;

1

they were well-to-do wool merchants and had paid their fines for not attending Church of England services. Their religion wasn't a crime, but if the authorities could find the man accused of being their chaplain, and somehow prove it, he would be guilty of a capital offence.

The militia stomped through the house, opening cupboards, banging on panelling, searching for priest holes. They wanted fires lit in every grate to smoke out anyone hiding up a hidden chimney ledge. The house had no such ingenious architecture. It had been built long before there was any need for such precautions.

The man they sought, Father William Bentney, was over seventy. It didn't require a whole troop of militia to flush him out. One man and his dog could have brought him in without a struggle. After all their energetic crashing about the great house, they found the frail bearded old fellow sitting in the summer house, wrapped in his dark cloak against the morning chill, where he'd been saying his morning Office. The clematis and wisteria had grown thick around the gazebo throughout the summer, obscuring him from view. When he heard the men march into the grounds, there was nowhere to run. He sat frozen on his bench, waiting, waiting, knowing he'd be found in good time and dragged off in the cart to await his fate. He'd never heard of any suspected priest had up for trial being found 'not guilty.'

He'd always known the risks. No priest sent to serve the English Mission could be unaware, but what puzzled William Bentney as he waited for the heavy tread of boots to search the garden, was the fact that he'd been in Leicester for over four decades, moving between known Catholic families. He'd always described himself as the Bentneys' 'head gardener', and had been careful t o travel with seeds or cuttings in his satchel, but the way people treated him, he reckoned most knew and let him be.

Why come for him now? Who had betrayed him? What had they stood to gain?

The psalm from his Office hit him with a new force:

> *With all my voice I cry to the Lord,*
> *with all my voice I entreat the Lord.*
> *I pour out my trouble before him;*
> *I tell him all my distress*
> *while my spirit faints within me*
> *(Psalm 141)*

1692

TEN YEARS LATER, LEICESTER

My eyes are ever fixed on the Lord,
for he releases my feet from the snare.
O look at me and be merciful,
for I am wretched and alone.

(Ps. 24)

She walked to the outskirts of the city, past the gossiping women at the Cank Streeet well, past the butchers' shambles, down the filthy lanes beyond Leicester gaol. Whenever she was stressed she had a habit of catching a strand of her curly, now greying, chestnut hair, twisting it round her finger, then trying to tuck it neatly under her cap. Her thick hair had no intention of being tamed and would soon escape to dangle fetchingly from her forehead down to tickle her neck. She had been twiddling those curls since she was a girl. This was not a visit she was looking forward to. Harry, a surly bear of a man and the senior gaoler, told her the criminals' cemetery was easy to find. He didn't seem to have much fellow feeling for his

4

charges, or for those who mourned them. She had met him every week for years, as she dropped off her basket of fresh laundry for the priest. Harry had grown to respect the old man. She'd come to see his gruffness as a shield; he couldn't carry on in his job if he let the world see how it affected him.

A rough untended patch bordered by a low picket fence. She knew there'd be no markers. Murderers and thieves deserved to be forgotten. His grave would have the freshest earth. It was close by the gate. Someone had made a crude cross, two strips of rough-hewn kindling laced together, to honour him. She scattered handfuls of white rose petals on the low mound. His roses, the ones he'd had planted and tended for years.

He was no thief, no murderer. He was a good man, old and doddery. She had wanted to look after him, spoil him with warm broth to build him up, his favourite cakes. Knit him warm scarves to keep out the cold. Old William was better than the father she couldn't remember, more like a kindly grandfather. What harm had he ever done anyone? Why did he have to waste away and die in the squalor of Leicester gaol?

Someone should have told her he was dying. She would have come. His gaolers weren't paid to send messages. She thought they might have let folks at the big house know, not her personally. She was nothing, just a servant. William had served them so long. They should have been told.

Maybe they were. Maybe after all the years he's been rotting away in his cell, after the scandal of his arrest, maybe they want the whole sad story to disappear and be forgotten. She wouldn't forget. She loved him.

She mustn't dally. The afternoon was growing darker, gloomier. Now that it had turned November, she wouldn't be surprised if there was a frost tonight. At any rate, the days were shorter and Belgrave Road was no place to be out and about when night fell. It was a good mile and a half to get back to the Hall. She tidied her unruly hair once more, caught the scent of roses on her hands, then pulled her shawl closer against a bitter wind, raising it up round her cap.

The weather had been mild enough through October. It was fortunate she'd saved the fragrant petals, even if they were as delicate as the old man. She'd wrapped them in a cloth in her basket. An errand to the chandler to stock up on more candles was a good enough excuse to slip into the city and pay her respects. Her leg was throbbing. A stumble on slippery kitchen steps back in the summer, a twisted ankle it seemed at the time. It still wasn't right. Maybe something had broken. Looked quite peculiar, crooked and swollen, swathed with a great rainbow of bruising colours.

Last year the walk into town would have been a pleasant stroll, now it was impossible. Tom hitched up the cart. She and Tom had both grown up working round Belgrave Hall. Tom was the village blacksmith's younger son, sandy-haired, of slim build and a man of few words. His older brother was keen to follow in his father's footsteps, but Tom wanted nothing better than to be out

6

in all weathers tending to plants. William said he had a natural gift for making things thrive. William had the ideas, Tom did the heavy work and had the callouses to prove it.

While William was held in gaol, except for the few weeks they kept him over in Derby for trial, it was Rebecca who looked after him, had kept bringing him fresh linen, the necessaries of life and whatever little treats from the kitchen she thought might cheer him up. A wise woman, she also brought ample treats for the two guards. These past few months what with her ankle slowing her down, Tom brought the basket instead. Rebecca was taking too long to heal. Tom saw the lines etched round her eyes from pain she tried to hide. At the gaol Tom could see his gentle mentor was getting weaker, but he was ever the optimist and didn't want to worry Rebecca. William might be eighty-three, but think of all the hardships and stresses he's managed to survive. He'll rally, Tom was sure of it. Until he didn't. Tom returned with the basket untouched.

Rebecca took it hard; Tom should have warned her, prepared her for this. He owed it to her to fetch the cart, and keep her company. She'd need to talk. He hoped the younger gaoler, Toby, would be on duty. He had befriended William, and he'd be the one to tell Becca about William's last days. But it was Harry who met Becca, not Toby. He'd been sent off to Derby to collect a ruffian to fill the vacant cell, a proper villian that Harry could delight in making miserable.

Her earliest memories were playing as a child on the floor of the Hall kitchen, watching her mother Molly cook for the grand folks. Molly was fairer than her daughter, with mousey brown fine hair prone to frizz in the kitchen steam. She was forever wiping her hands on her long apron, often as not because they were covered in flour. Molly's pastry was a little bit of heaven and much praised. The offcuts her mother called 'trattlins' Molly used to spread with a dollop of jam and roll up to cook alongside the pies. The trattlins were all for Rebecca.

It was William who told her stories to keep her out of harm's way when the food preparation became more hectic. He was the one who taught her to read., sitting next to him at the kitchen table. She was seven when he arrived. Back then his beard was still brown. He wasn't like the other labourers. His hands were clean, soft, more like her mother's. His clothes were simple, 'honest garb' her mother would have said. Not fine silks like the master, but not grimy, patched and worn through like a farmhand. He was something in between.

He was also something special. Even a child could figure that out. Even though he was not an old man, he was called 'Father' and spoke proper. He was an educated man, there was no hiding it. He might try to pick up local expressions, but they never quite sounded right and natural when he said them. Molly was pleased Father William was spending time with her 'Becca.

On fine days he'd walk the child around the gardens telling her about the various plants, helping her to learn their names. Father William didn't do the planting himself, he oversaw the work. Tom was the lad who'd come into the kitchen glistening with sweat, wondering if Molly might have a fresh batch of scones that needed sampling or a jug of cider going begging. He could always make 'Becca laugh. Tom and Molly spoke pure Leicester, which is how she knew Father William was different.

Whenever she'd heard the master or mistress speak, they too sounded different, said their words clearly, but they had a way of speaking that kept her at arm's length. Their eyes maybe were kindly and well-meaning, but their manner was like they'd catch fleas off her if they got too close. They made her feel she could never understand anything as complicated as their lives. She wondered if any of them could manage to serve up the elaborate dinners her 'uneducated' mother prepared. Oh, they were grateful, full of praise and all, but Molly and her daughter knew their place in the scheme of things.

William didn't make Becca feel less, less gifted or less valued or valuable. When there was just the immediate family to dine, he would eat with them. If there were any visitors, he'd often eat back with staff in the kitchen. He was soft-spoken, not like the master who could often be heard shouting. If he was thumping papers on his desk, it was not wise to disturb him. Mother said the master had a lot of business worries. He had to provide for the whole household, so Becca was to be good and not play too loudly.

Belgrave Hall was a sizeable household to maintain, the largest edifice in the village. The taxman counted ten chimneys to assess its rates. The taxman didn't have to clean ten grates. Rebecca did, as a child. The master, William Byerley, had done well enough in the wool trade to move out of the cramped city and set up home in this more impressive setting. They were lucky. That was back in 1641, before the Civil War wreaked havoc on Leicester.

This ancient mansion house adjoined the turnpike road, and from Leicester, was the first good house on the left in the village. The end adjoining the turnpike was older than the main body of the house. There are clues from the from the fragments of arches, semi-arches and carved stone heads like those projecting from the inside of church walls, that this might be the remains of a chapel or chantry. The house was originally owned and occupied by the Hastings family.

It had a particular attraction for the Byerleys: it had a Catholic chapel in a large garret. The Hastings of Braunstone had once been a Catholic family too, but had dropped out of the struggle during the long years of proscription. They could no longer afford the fines. Perhaps they were not displeased that their chapel would remain in use and treasured by the new occupants.

The altar was separated from the east end by oak balustrades. Mats were provided for worshippers to kneel on. Over the altar hung a painting of the Crucifixion, with a painting on either side, very dark and old, not easily made out, but probably of the original donors or owners of the house. At the back of the altar table, which was fixed, was a cupboard, blue and gold and marbled red and white, which was used as the tabernacle. Over the altar and cupboard was suspended a canopy in crimson in the centre with the letters 'IHS' surrounded by golden embroidery. Curtains match the canopy.

Downstairs in the great hall there are half a dozen old family portraits. Rebecca had no idea who they were, she just dusted the frames and washed the floor as she was told. The South window is decorated with stained glass portraying a Scripture scene, the crowning of Queen Esther. It has recently been repaired at the bottom with bits of unmatched fragments, but the central figures are finely executed and expressive. Two of the remaining south windows have coats of arms. The north side hall door features a stone shield embossed with the coat of arms of the Byerleys.

During the Byerley's tenure, following William Bentney's designs, Belgrave Hall featured a summer house in the garden which one visitor decribed as having 'curious plasterwork'. Its ceiling has ornate wooden carvings of a variety of foliage, oak branches with acorns, vines with grapes, and the like. The garden, which lies chiefly in front of the house, is on an elevated spot. It has become an ornament to the village. It has been laid out with low hedges of thyme and box. The walks are always kept in good order, and the flowerbeds maintain a display of splendor throughout the changing seasons.

It was a difficult world for the Byerley family even though Leicester was relatively safe. Leicester, by and large, let people be. Religious toleration was more generally welcomed than in most of the country. There were a large number of respectable dissenters. Penal laws which were aimed primarily at Catholics were not rigorously enforced. A recusant was a Roman Catholic who had been detected, reported to the authorities, taken into court and convicted of the crime of recusancy. In time even a Protestant Dissenter might be accused; some offences were no worse than neglect of churchgoing.

Belgrave Hall stood next to the church of St. Peter, which was on the town side of the manor house. It would have taken no great genius to notice that no one from the Hall attended. St. Peter's dated from the 13th century, although there were a few features remaining from the 12th century church. The nave, aisles and tower arch and lancet date from the 13th century. The chancel was rebuilt in the 14th. The clerestory and the upper stage of the tower date from the 16th century. Becca sensed these close neighbours were friendly. She helped feed the builders the Byerleys funded to repair the church at various times.

If anyone had a decent income, the authorities were on the lookout to see if they showed up for Church of England services. Not all lay members of the Roman Catholic underground movement were discovered. Even if they were discovered, not all were reported. Sometimes, even if they were reported, it did not go to court proceedings. Even if it went that far, not all laymen and women proceded against were convicted.

There were mixed motives. Reluctance to harm one's neighbour or to offend one's landlord. There was reluctance on the part of Church of England clergy to admit there were papists in their parishes. Official reports tended to underestimate the numbers, basing figures on only those convicted and omitting any under sixteen.

In 1676 there were probably 1,100 Catholics in Leicestershire. The government fined the better off to win revenue; harrassing the indigent was useless. The lists in the House of Lords of reported Catholics probably only accounts for half the true number. A low government figure also suited some politicians who wished a policy of repression to succeed.

From 1622 the family started to acquire property in Belgrave. By 1641 they bought the Hall with its elaborate chapel. A succession of Franciscan chaplains served the area and found accomodation at the Hall. The Byerley's only son, Charles, was then seven and his father sought out a Jesuit chaplain to act as his tutor, although he'd describe the priest's position as 'Head gardener' if anyone inquired. The priest would be wise enough never to be caught up in any political discussions. Wise enough, too, never to be caught with the tools of his trade, a chalice, wine and other Mass requirements, when travelling between various Leicestershire villages.

The Jesuits had a preference for serving the well-to-do, those more likely to wield influence and power. They were known for setting up schools for boys. William Byerley thought his enhanced status might attract a suitable Jesuit missionary. However, national events intervened: the Civil War. All chances of acquiring a tutor would have to wait until peace was restored.

It was not until 1652, two years after the execution of Charles I, that it was deemed safe enough for Father William Bentney to take up his place at Belgrave Hall. With a nod and a wink, most folk in Leicester knew exactly what he was, and let him get on with it. Father William served his flock without drawing attention to himself. He was well liked and trusted, a quiet drinker down the pub, a good listener.

He was no threat to anyone.

Which is why thirty years later Rebecca wondered who set the authorities on him? Rebecca wanted answers. Who stood to gain? Why, after so many years of tolerance?

1641

LEICESTER BEFORE THE CIVIL WAR

The Lord will guard you from evil,
he will guard your soul.
The Lord will guard your going and your coming
both now and forever.

(Ps. 120)

When the Byerleys were preparing to move up to the Hall, they decided it was time to acquire another cook. The hiring fair for servants took place three days before and three days after the feast of St. Michael. Open air 'statues', men and maids, lined down the streets. Each prospective employee displayed a symbol of their skills. A waggoner stood with a knot of whipcord in his hand, a shepherd with a bit of wool, a thresher with a few wheat ears. A cowman held on to a swatch from a cow's tail.

Molly was eighteen, and as good a cook as any fine gentleman could wish for. She didn't want to be hired by just anyone, made to do all rough work. She wanted to demonstrate her talent. Just a taste of something light and lovely. She'd stand her ground holding a small platter of Valentine buns. They came out of the oven well risen and golden from their glaze. No one else would dream of cooking them in autumn.

As she was just heading out to secure her pitch, Molly's mother hugged her and tied a small medallion around her neck. 'What's this?'

'Just something to make sure you get a decent employer.'

'What, some lucky charm? Where did you get this? You don't believe in luck or charms.'

'Not exactly a charm. It's something I was given by a pilgrim returned from Walsingham. If a gentleman comments on it, knows what it is, he'll be a pious man, a good man most like. Not the sort to take advantage. Then let him try those cakes.'

And so it proved. When Byerley passed Molly, he smiled at the comely lass as she curtseyed. He asked to look at her medallion, understood the coded hope for a household that kept to the Old Faith. He offered the hiring penny before he'd even tasted the Valentine treats. Michaelmas fairs usually hired for the twelvemonth. Molly would never return.

Molly was to take her instructions from Betty, who'd been in charge of the Byerley kitchen for 'donkey's years', she told her. Betty was a force to be reckoned with , and pure Leicester. Her ample figure suggested that either she was a good cook, or quite a few left-overs found their way onto her dinner plate. Perhaps both. A scullery girl, a scullion, from the village was no longer enough help. Betty was a tad breathless and preferred sitting at the kitchen table barking out orders than standing fussing over a delicate sauce. She knew exactly how the masters liked their meals, how they celebrated festivals, and who to get supplies from.

It didn't take long for Betty to assess that Molly would do nicely. She was a quick learner and pleasant with it. Not, so far as she could see, inclined to be 'mardy' like so many young girls. No sulks, no moods, no back chat. A good choice.

Betty wasn't the only one to approve. Ben, the millar's son, soon spotted the new arrival. He delivered enormous sacks of flour to the Hall, hefting them down off his wagon laid across his broad shoulders. Molly was told to fetch him cider for his trouble. He caught her wrist and begged for a bit of bread and cheese to go with it. He winked at Betty, as much to say his hunger wasn't entirely focused on the food. He was a good-looking lad and he knew it, probably had a string of girls sighing after him in the village. Molly'd seen his type before.

'Watch yourself with that one, me duck,' warned Betty when he'd gone, 'Don't you go being another notch on his belt now.'

Molly laughed away her warning, reassuring her she had the measure of him. That didn't stop her gazing after his wagon, though, or delighting at the sight of his tousled dark curls and fine sculpted body whenever he dropped by. Which, it seemed to Betty, was a lot more often than ever he used to.

1652

ELEVEN YEARS LATER, AFTER THE CIVIL WAR

Be a rock of refuge for me,
a mighty stronghold to save me,
for you are my rock, my stronghold.
For your name's sake, lead me and guide me.
(Ps.30)

It was late September when the wagon drew up and dropped off the new priest and several fruit crates and a hessian sack which contained his teaching supplies and his earthly goods. He'd have time to settle in before the liveliness of the Christmas festivities got under way. Betty had looked after the previous Franciscans. She liked some better than others. Those that had a sense of humour she spoiled, those that understood her gruffness to be affection. Twenty years back the Order had appointed a Guardian of Leicester to look after Catholics in the district. Father Thomas Smith O.F.M.Rec. was the latest one. He always appreciated a good meal when he dropped by.

Father William arrived from his former posting in

Hertfordshire, as the long awaited tutor. Eleven years after his training in France, he was a young looking forty-three, and not at all sure what challenges Leicester would offer. He was slimmer than the previous lot and Betty decided he needed mothering. 'You need feeding up,' she announced, 'that southern muck hasn't done you any favours. You need proper food to build up your strength.'

He smiled nervously, politely. He'd always been wiry, strong as an ox with broad shoulders, but never the sort to fill out.

'Where do you hail from, where are your family?'

'Cheshire', he mumbled reluctantly, 'dairy farmers over Nantwich way.' Indeed, he had the sturdy- boned features of farming folk, a long, ruddy face.that creased easily into a warm offer of friendship.He looked a man who knew which end of a cow to milk.This wasn't the austere, aloof scholar they expected from the Jesuits. He didn't seem cut of their elite cloth. Perhaps that was why he was sent, to be out of the way in a forgettable, unpromising posting. Father William had to admit, ' I don't know much about Leicester...someone at Heythrop joked I'd be fed nothing but beans, and folk had better keep upwind of me.'

Molly giggled, 'Oh, that's the county alright, 'bean-belly Leicestershire'! Betty agreed, 'Shake a Leicestershire yeoman by the collar, and you'll hear the beans rattle in his belly,' that's how they tease us right enough. I've heard other folks use 'em as food for horses and hogs, but hereabouts they eat them green and turn a fair penny selling them to their neighbours too.'

19

William looked as if he might himself turn a shade of green at the thought. 'Oh, don't you fret, we'll not feed you beans, leastways, not every day!' Betty cackled, 'Can't have you embarrassing yourself on the altar now, can we?'

'Thank you, Betty, I'm most grateful for your concern for my dignity', he retorted, grinning. The new chaplain had a hearty deep laugh, which relaxed the atmosphere. He fitted into the kitchen banter and was a pleasure to have around, no problem at all.

It was a few mornings later, after Mass and morning prayers in the chapel and after the family had been fed, Father William slipped into the kitchen for the hearty breakfast that Betty delighted in serving him. In between mouthfuls, he tried to strike up a conversation with Betty, partly to stop her loading yet more food onto his plate. 'So why is this village called 'Belgrave'? Is there some French history...'bel, belle'? It's a charming site, well enough.'

Betty took the bait. 'Beautiful or not, that's not what the country folk'll tell you. It's all about a giant, some say a devil, named Bell. Once when he was in a rather jolly mood he decided to take three enormous leaps. At a place, which ever afterwards called Mountsorrel, he mounted his sorrel horse and leapt a mile. He landed in a place called One Leap, what we call Wanlip now. Next he leapt another mile, to a place called Burstall, because there it was both he and his horse burst. He lost his girth, and his horse. His third leap was also for a mile, but the violence of the effort and the shock of it killed him, and there he was buried. Bell's grave, or Bel-grave it's all the same', Betty gave a mock bow at the end of her tale.

'Fantastic, great fun with the village names!'

'Now we do have proper French names, like Beaumanor up the road, and of course 'Bel-voir' castle, but you must remember to call it 'Beaver', else they'll know you're not from round here.They've a priest up there as well, you know.'

When Father Bentney started as chaplain, William Byerley, the head of the household was not much older than the priest, but already a widower. His first wife, Jane, had died two months after giving birth to their son. The child, named after his father, did not survive past his first birthday. Wives spent their child -bearing years almost continually great-bellied or recovering from a birth. Miscarriages, babies who did not survive, were common.

Elizabeth, William's second wife, had not managed a biblical quiverful of offspring , but there was a son and heir Charles, a young man of eighteen, no longer requiring a tutor, and his sister Anne, already nineteen and in hopes of soon finding a suitable husband. Elizabeth was still young enough to have more children, and no doubt her fierce prayerfulness in chapel may well be focused on that hope. Elizabeth was, William guessed, near the end of her child-bearing years. They could certainly afford a larger brood, but that further blessing didn't seem likely.

The chapel was not for the exclusive use of the family and members of the staff. A couple tenant farmers, labourers, villagers, the widow Dawson, the miller and his family, and others, the faithful of modest means, clambered up to the garret. Always at night, with the curtains drawn, always careful to admit only those known to the community. They came and left round the back, by the barn, so as not to be noticed. Molly made sure they had a nice slice of fruit cake and a cup of tea before they set off home.

Once the new priest felt comfortable in the village, he joined Molly on her errands into town. It was a cramped wooden town, largely confined within old and crumbling medieval walls. Newer suburbs and a few stray houses had sprawled out beyond, but none substantial. There was a shortage of timber to repair or build new homes because the forest had gone when Charles I enclosed it over thirty years back. The able-bodied poor had found work carrying firewood from the forest on their backs, but this option was no longer possible. The corporation decreed that only freemen were allowed to engage in retail trade. This, they claimed, was to maintain high standards of craftsmanship and not have local goods undercut by goods from elsewhere where wages were lower and quality less reliable. There was an increasing number of people who were not freemen, not wanted as apprentices and who had to live somewhere. There was a meagre dole for the workless and a protected standard of living for sheltered industries. A scheme was being tried out to 'set the poor on work' by having them knit or weave caps and stockings in their cottages.

Trying to sound more positive about her hometown, Molly showed off the Town Library in the Town Hall, Wyggeston's Hospital and the Free Grammar School, built from the salvaged remnants of old St. Peter's church. 'There aren't many grand buildings to show you, but you can't miss the 'Lord's Place', the Earls of Huntingdon over in High Street. That's the Hastings family who run everything…not the Braunstone ones who are poor as church mice, or as good as.'

'How did Leicester fare during the war? I know when the Roundheads were besieging Oxford, Prince Rupert decided to set on Leicester to distract them, divert their energy.'

'Oh, he did that alright. The Earl of Stamford had had a garrison in town for three years, with little bother. The town was mostly in favour of the Parliamentary side, but not keen to be torn up by all-out war. We had no serious way to defend ourselves, just crumbling walls. It only took a few days. The garrison refused to surrender, so Rupert sent the troops in and it was pretty fierce they say.'

'How was it out in Belgrave? Did the Hall come under attack?'

'No, just raided for provisions, by both sides. They helped themselves to pigs and chickens mainly. One of the Roundheads took umbridge with that stained glass window in the great hall, Esther, and lobbed a stone through it, but we were lucky. Mind you, we kept the chapel curtains drawn so as not to draw attention to it. No, we were lucky, not like the townsfolk.'

'I can see quite a few rough efforts at patching damage. Looks too much for cannonfire, if the siege was only a couple of days.'

'No, it wasn't cannons did this, it was the saltpetre men. It's not a big town, so when two armies fought in the streets, ordinary folk were killed, most were robbed in the chaos. Then those men came, looking for the stuff to make their gunpowder. The doings of animals and humans that makes saltpetre. The King's men claimed the right to barge into private property with warrants, smashing up barnyards and homes, digging up mud floors, pulling down mud walls, trying to get dove droppings or sheep shit. Since the poorest homes had the best pickings, they suffered the most. You got battered or worse if you tried to protect your house. The whole business left a pretty sour taste for the King's cause, I can tell you.

'Mind you, two weeks later, it was all change. When the King was back in Leicester he was a prisoner after losing at Naseby. They put him up in the Angel, no doubt you'll be stopping there now and again. It's a fine inn. Course there were some scores to settle. The Roundheads set fires, we could see the smoke from the Hall. The Countess of Devonshire's mansion burned for days, her thanks for supporting the King.'

The priest had been given some background information on his new posting. The county was first and foremost a sheep-farming and wool producing area. Molly showed him the Byerley's warehouse. 'Sheep round hereabouts grow long wool, best for worsted cloth ,' Molly informed him, ' but our lot gets shipped over East Anglia way to manufactories there. From things I've heard, that's where the money is.'

Father William asked his host at dinner about the local wool. 'The best broadcloth is at present coming in from Flanders, but wool merchants over here are trying

24

to compete. Unfortunately, Leicester can't. Broadcloth needs a short wool and reliable water power for the fulling. Leicester has the wrong sheep, the wrong sort of waterways...' he sighed. William felt he'd broached a sore topic. The wool trade in Leicester and the Byerley's business, while profitable enough, now seemed well in decline. He secretly wondered how secure their future might be.

The priest was given a letter to deliver in town, requesting the Corporation's musicians to come to Belgrave Hall to liven up the Christmas festivities. The town fathers hired five minstrels, 'waits', and decked them in official livery. Their job was to watch (or 'wait') through the night for fire or foe. They were of course required to provide music up in the minstrels' gallery in the Guildhall for all municipal functions, and twice daily all through the year to play in a public place for the pleasure of the people. Market Day was Saturday; they should be easy enough to spot playing out in front of the Angel Inn.

It was not an onerous task and Father William soon found his way to the lively market. Ben was just finishing his deliveries and spotted the newcomer. He beckoned him over and the pair decided delivering letters or sacks of flour was definitely thirsty work, and a pint was in order. The Angel was doing a brisk business what with the Saturday crowds. With its low ceiling, dark paneling, and welcome fire, it was a great escape from a piercing North wind.

A whiskery old chap was tucked in the corner. His white hair was wild, his eyes bright and cheerful, thanking a friend who'd just bought him a drink. By the look of him, the Jesuit guessed, a man who'd laid claim to that warm corner for a good few decades and who was part of the furniture. His right to that spot was well earned, Father William soon saw, when a fiddle was tucked up under his chin. The notes tickled the air, a little jarring those chords at first, then the pace built up into a fine jig. A penny whistle sprouted from someone's jacket and joined in. In minutes the room had men clapping, tapping their feet, everyone smiling.

Ben had never seen the priest so animated. It was good to see him relax, not be so serious and earnest all the time. He watched how fascinated the newcomer seemed, fixed on the old man. When the music paused for him to sup his brew, Father William found a stool next to him and struck up a conversation. Ben couldn't hear what what was said, but saw the old man hand over his fiddle. William stroked it with care, praised it, he thought, then tucked it under his own chin, plucking a few strings tentatively. 'Go on, me lad, see what you can do. See if it likes you.'

It liked him well enough. A ballad, low and sad, with a clear sweetness in the notes he found brought the noisy banter to a hush. When the song finished, Father William was cheered. Another pint found its way to his side. Ben was told to bring his new friend round again, 'Friday nights we could use another fiddler, Jake could do with someone to spell him, more time for him to sup up!' The priest said he'd happily come, and bring his own fiddle, if Jake could teach him to play those lively reels. He only knew a few old ballads, the tearful ones his mother used to sing. The deal was done.

'Why didn't you let them up at the hall know about your music?'

'Music was just for fun when I was growing up. Everyone in the family could join in. Picking up a fiddle came natural, like learning to walk. I was never taught properly, just watched and listened, and copied what I could remember. It's not the kind of music grand folk like, so I didn't think the Byerleys would be interested.'

'Don't you be so sure. Maybe not to impress their fancy cousins, but you'd be surprised how much fun that quiet old place can muster over Christmas. Get up some reels with our Jake and I promise you'll be well appreciated at the Hall by Twelfth Night. I can't wait to see the look on their faces when their pious gardener starts them all dancing!'

Molly of course was in on the secret. Friday nights Ben tapped on the kitchen door and William slipped out unnoticed with his violin tucked under his great coat, off for his music lessons with Jake. Ben was glad of an excuse to be off to the pub, and even gladder to be returning to Betty's kitchen afterwards. Molly'd have a few cheese cobs, maybe a slice of pie for them both. They never objected to another mug or two of something to keep the chill off, either.

Upstairs, the master of the Hall could hear their laughter. The first few Friday nights he thought he might have a problem on his hands, a holy man too fond of his drink, too fond to be careful. He was considering having a word with him when the sound of the jollity struck him: that loud throaty laugh was Ben's, not the priest's. Father William was the lower voice, calmer, but definitely enjoying himself. Perhaps that word could wait. His wife might think every minute should be spent in prayer, but that made life awfully dull. A little joy now and again was good for the soul he reckoned.

The priest heard all about how Ben had relentlessly pursued Molly until she finally agreed to marry him. Betty had kept up her muttered warnings about his wandering eyes, but Molly had refused to listen. Finding a place to live had been the only problem, a place near enough to the mill and the big house, so Molly could keep her position. Mr. Byerley was the landlord for the cottages in the village. When Widow Craddock died, the couple had finally been able to set up home together. Their daughter Rebecca was born the following year, just after the Parliamentarians recaptured Leicester back from the Royalists in 1645.

A routine of sorts was evolving, a way for William to fulfill his vocation and also prove useful to the running of the Hall. He guided Charles in his reading, improved his Latin and theology in the mornings. Charles worked with his father in the afternoons, learning the business. Anne had reached the limit of her education much earlier, not from any lack of ability, but it was her vocation to run a household and bear children as a dutiful wife. Merchants' wives were cannier than fine ladies; they often were almost considered business partners. Elizabeth may well have been tutoring Anne on economics behind the boudoir door, to help her support her future husband's prospects, but Anne's preparation for adult responsibilities was not William's concern, beyond of course for her spiritual welfare.

Father William hadn't heard whether or not there was a music master, and certainly didn't feel qualified to offer his services. Afternoons he usually spent on various visits to the elderly, house-bound, or those known to be ill or injured. He carried a basket of provisions and often would be accompanied by the mistress of the Hall, Elizabeth. Good works and a rigorous attention to her prayer book were the how she filled her days after briskly delegating household tasks to servants. Elizabeth was pale and slender. Bringing two children into the world had not filled her out. She looked drawn and rarely smiled. Her hands were long and thin, always cold. She wrung them constantly and wore gloves whenever possible.

As the days lengthened into December, there was a great deal to be done to prepare for Christmas. William was told in no uncertain terms to be clear of the kitchen and the farmyard out back when it was time to slaughter the pigs. A messy business, with every bit needing its own way of being preserved. 'Chittering pies' would be filled with minced pork, covered with pastry shaped like a pig, with currant eyes. A treat the children loved. The finest cuts would be roasted for the feast. Throughout the twelve days all levels of society would be welcomed into the Great Hall, with set days for different groups, local villagers and tenanted farmers and the miller, another day for business associates, another for extended family, including their grand cousins. The Byerleys had been entertaining on this lavish scale for twelve years. They knew the duty of hospitality, and how to impress.

When Betty and Molly were first shown the guest list,

they begged a day or two between each wave, to give them time to clear up one lot and get the next huge groaning board ready. They had a small army of helpers, a raft of scullions, a couple of apprentice butchers and bakers all getting in each other's way. Betty swore she'd take to her bed for a week if she managed to survive past Epiphany, and she was only half joking. Extra kitchen girls from the village were brought in.

Father William was asked to help Tom Moore, who lived nearby in Bird's Close, to take the cart and restock the woodshed. They'd be getting through more than usual when the festivities started. Most of the bigger logs had been cut a few months back, to give them time to dry out, but fresh kindling would need less time. Tom and William were also expected to fetch greenery to decorate the hall and chapel. William had spotted some fine holly laden with berries adjacent to the Hall in Townsend Close, so all in all, the titular gardener would be earning his keep.

William was also delegated to visit the housebound with Christmas hampers from the Byerleys. It wasn't all one way. Most of the farmers brought produce as offerings towards the feast, some caught fish. Widow Smith had a few jars of pickles for the big house, and Anne Devonshire, known for her fine needlework, had fashioned another kneeler for the chapel.

The festivities began slowly, quietly, with a late night Mass on Christmas Eve, not quite as late as midnight, but only for the regular faithful. Of course they left after a hearty glass of punch and treats Molly had set out as a buffet. Most would return and mingle with the rest of their neighbours for the open house. That was the first day the minstrels were booked. One corner of the Hall had been set aside for them and a temporary raised dias built. Benches lined the walls, the long dining table had been placed to one side to clear the centre. The fire was well built up. Hot pokers were warming mugs of punch with a sizzle. The smell of roast meats and fish filled the air. Candlelight flattered everyone, no matter how humble, how wizened. This was the best of the gatherings, surrounded by friends and neighbours, with less tension, less need to stand on ceremony.

When the dining had finished, the minstrels struck up. A space was cleared for dancing. Having had a fair sample of the punch, most were merry and a few in high colour even before the exertion of whirling one's partner across the floor. After a pause in the music, the fiddler raised his bow. He looked like he was just adjusting the bowstring tension, but it was a signal. Hidden in the crowd in the opposite corner was William, ready with his fiddle. This was the moment he'd been practising for. The minstrel played a line; the other musicians smiled and held back. From his corner the priest stepped from the crowd and repeated the refrain.

The pair of fiddlers echoed each other several times, each time more intricately, as Father William gradually walked forward, the crowd clearing a path for him. When he stepped onto the dias, all the minstrels joined in. They switched to playing 'Strip the Willow', a favourite Leicester dance. Partners lined up ready to hook elbows and twirl. The room gave a cheer and clapped. The Byerleys looked

31

stunned at first, but Elizabeth was actually seen to be smiling and clapping. While the dancers caught their breath, William played one of his soulful ballads, then slipped through the crowd. He returned a few moments later, minus the fiddle. The Byerleys came over to praise his virtuosity, somewhat surprised he had kept it a secret. He explained his lack of formal training, and assured them both that he wouldn't be giving any more unscheduled performances this holiday.

Father William kept out of the way for the business associates' feast, and for the wider family gathering. They were much more sedate affairs, a fair bit of networking, a smattering of gossip, the usual non too subtle showing off, and a considerable amount of politics.

In the transformed world of Cromwell's new government, the Mayors and Justices were expected to enforce the ideal of a uniform and moderate puritanism in a society that was not wholly in tune with such beliefs. They had to fine people for working or allowing their children to play on the Lord's day, for playing 'shove-grote', for ringing church bells outside agreed times, for drinking the king's health. They had the power to impound heretical books and had some Quakers arrested.

It was only two years since the king had been executed. A once seemingly stable world had had its certainties swept away. In light of this uneasy atmosphere, the dress code was more restained than in past years. Far less lace, more subdued colours. Less ornate hair styles. The Puritans would not have approved of any sort of card games or dice.

For over a hundred years Catholic priests had had to

conceal their identity. One fellow Jesuit of William's, John Gerard, some fifty years earlier, wrote that he was forced at his lodging to play cards as part of his disguise. His hostess chided him for being 'like a courtier' for being at the game so long. It was an odd business playing with Catholics, Gerard found, because every player got his or her money back at the end, with the loser having to say an *Ave Maria* for every counter returned.

The Byerleys knew better than to risk card playing with the new regime in charge.

1653

GARDENING

> *Praise the Lord from the earth,*
> *all mountains and hills,*
> *all fruit trees and cedars,*
> *Let them praise the name of the Lord. (Ps. 148)*

Late one morning, William Byerley unexpectedly dropped in on Charles' morning lessons. He gave cursory approval of Charles' work on Aquinas, then gestured that he wanted a quiet word with the priest

'I'm off to do a spot of fishing this afternoon. The rights to this stretch of the Soar came with the Hall, and I don't make good use of them often enough. I was rather hoping you'd join me.'

Although the cleric had never tried fishing before, he willingly agreed. It promised to be a pleasant diversion from his usual routine and the Spring weather was particularly inviting. He also suspected the master had more on his mind than rod and reel. The walk past the church was suitable for sketching, dappled light filtered by hanging elms and willows, shading the serpentine river. The mill was just visible off through the trees. They were

34

on a quiet,narrow lane, that ran close to the riverbank, well away from the more traveled road by the Hall. They chose a spot under a willow to spread their rug and unload their tackle.

Once the basic points were explained and hooks baited, the pair stepped into a clearing to teach the novice how to cast. He was initially ungainly and a good few tangles needed sorting, but eventually his patient tutor declared he had the knack. The peace of the setting, birdsong, the placid stream, and the welcome warmth of the May sun on their backs, relaxed them both. This was the intimacy Byerley had sought to broach difficult thoughts. The lord of the manor was only a few years older than the cleric, but his fuller waistline showed he was not acquainted with self-denial. His business worries might have lined his brow and started to grey his hair, but had not dented his appetite.

He spoke of what he had heard; the priest shared what gossip swirled around town, admitting that grumblings and underlying suspicion of anything that veered towards popery made it more uncomfortable to move about in public. On Ben's advice he'd let his carefully trimmed stylish goatee fill out acoss his jawline; a fuller beard looked less elitist, less noteworthy. A better disguise. He was uneasy about his Fridays at the Angel, and kept finding excuses to let Ben go on his own.

'Probably wise,' Byerley muttered. He too was anxious; trade was very slow. No one wants to place orders with the future so uncertain. Can't trust getting payment, can't risk moving goods from the warehouses. Soldiers no

35

longer employed in war found their skills transferable as highwaymen.He didn't want to speak of his concerns at the dinner table, in front of the family.

'There's another matter you should be aware of,' Byerley paused, it's Anne. It's time she was wed. She's had an offer. A widower, Humphrey Wharton from London. He was here over Christmas. He's a fair bit older than Anne, but he's a good man from what I've heard, and he and Anne seemed amenable to the match. We've started negotiating the details..but that's neither here nor there.

'My worry is Elizabeth. With Anne off to London, the poor woman will have nothing but her prayers to fill her life. She'll wear holes in her dresses kneeling so long! It's a fine thing to be so devout, but there's a line, I reckon, a dangerous line, when it can be too much. But perhaps you don't agree?'

'I've seen Elizabeth praying for hours, of course, I have. Her heart is pure and her faith strong…but I have noted her tension, too, her hands wringing and a sad stillness about her. Her eyes light up when she's with Anne. That's her hope it seems. Losing her will be a great blow.'

'Indeed.'

'May I make a suggestion? I have an idea that might help, a project to do with my 'gardening' responsibilities. I've managed to get hold of some notes and sketches of Sir Thomas Tresham's gardens…'

'Wait a minute, the Tresham that was involved in the Gunpowder Plot?'

'No, that was his son. The father designed splendid

houses and gardens using hidden religious symbolism and numerology. Lyveden Garden is the one I want to show Elizabeth. I thought if we could borrow some of his ideas, on a much more modest scale of course, here at Belgrave Hall, well it might give her a new focus.'

'Certainly she could do with something else to think about. With every passing year the sight of that empty cradle in our room weighs heavier on her, a guilt she carries no matter how I try and tell her she's nothing to feel guilty about…Can you reassure her? She'd listen to you. Can you help to distract those dark thoughts?'

'I promise to do my best, sir. A little more fresh air and some building plans to fuss over might lift her spirits, especially if there's a hidden meaning in it all.'

'Building plans? What have you got in mind? I can't commit to anything ambitious with things the way they are now. I thought you were just talking about a few fancy flower beds. What exactly are you proposing?'

'Nothing more than a summer house, a place where Elizabeth can come to read her prayerbook. The garden would be constructed with gravel paths between hedges of thyme or box, with benches here and there. Hedges in a geometric pattern, reflecting the design and order of the universe. Lyveden's based on the Passion and on the Virgin Mary, red flowers to symbolise the Passion, white for Mary's purity. Tresham alternated white roses with raspberry plants or strawberries underplanted beneath roses. It could be quite literally a feast for the senses. Mind you, Sir Thomas did have an orchard of over three hundred fruit trees approached by an avenue of walnut trees, but perhaps we could venture a limited selection of fruit trees over by Townsend Close? '

'The flowers and a few fruit trees are no problem, a fine suggestion. That front lawn needs something certainly.If you were seen to be constructing this new plan, your role as gardener would be more credible to all and sundry too, which is no bad thing. Why a summer house? Sounds like a fair expense, if it's done in good taste. '

'Well, actually Sir Thomas built a whole banqueting hall with the bay to the entrance porch having five sides each five feet long, to signify March 25th and December 25th, the Annunciation and Christmas. I thought a five sided summer house was a manageable compromise, and something we all could enjoy, as the centrepiece of our geometric hedged paths, but if you feel it's too much outlay, I understand.'

'No, no, compared to a banqueting hall, I guess a summer house is small beer. I think we can risk a summer house. Put your plans to Elizabeth, I think it might well inspire her. Head on over to Beaumanor to get some cuttings. I hear their gardens are more ambitious. Never had time to give it much thought before, when we lived in the town.'

They stayed by the willow until the afternoon shadows lengthened. It had been good. Byerley walked beside the priest silently for some way, wondering if he should risk a more personal question. 'Tell me if I am intruding, but you have seemed a bit quieter of late. Is it the talk of Cromwell, or is something else worrying you?'

Bentney paused, his eyes tight shut, his face taut.

They'd reached a ruined stone bridge. The priest stopped and sat on a tumbled block. 'I've had word that my father has died. It's a heavy thing to keep to oneself. We're supposed to cut off all past family life when we sign up for the English Mission. For their safety as much as ours.I ache to be back home, to comfort my mother, but daren't go, must not go. I know that, but my head is there all the same. All the prayers and Masses won't stop me longing to rush back. My father hated lawyers, never trusted them, never wanted anyone knowing his business. His estates are under threat of being sequestered. They could take it into their heads to imprison my mother if she can't afford the fines. I'm desperate to know what is happening, but the least hint of what has become of me puts her in danger… I'm sorry, I shouldn't trouble you with this, I shouldn't speak of such things…' His voice trailed into silence, muttering his apologies.

Byerley put his arm round him, reassuring him he knew how to keep secrets. 'The death of a father is a hard thing to carry on your own. My father died when I was twenty-five. I had family around, cousins, aunts, uncles, but I never felt so alone. Mother had gone before him, so it was down to me to make decisions, sort it all. I was numb and wanted the world to stop…You need to escape our household, find some time away from all that hubub, maybe say you're coming out here to do a spot of fishing. No one will bother you out here. No one will ever know why, I promise you.'

Bentney nodded, gratefully. His eyes were moist and he was unable to speak. To fill the silence, Byerley mused aloud that he too had a distrust of lawyers, but he'd found one that was better than most. 'Sorting wills and inheritance is a tricky business for us these days, certainly, and there's no telling what new laws will turn up to trap us, but so far I reckon I've managed to entail everything so Elizabeth and Charles are not in jeopardy too...yes, yes,I pray it holds valid when the time comes.'

The pair rarely had time to slip away from the Hall to speak freely in the coming months, but would exchange knowing looks when they passed in corridors or across the dinner table. Byerley often noted the absence of the tackle creel from the boot room and smiled, reassured to see the lone mourner had taken him up on his offer.

The garden transformation for Belgrave Hall began to take shape. The foundations were laid for the central summer house and the wooden framework soon rose up with its hexagonal outline. Elizabeth had the idea to incorporate a carved inner ceiling with a trailing vine motif. It would echo the actual vines they planned to surround the gazebo, but for her it would symbolise Christ's description of himself as the true vine,

> 'I am the vine, you are the branches.
> He who abides in me, and I in him, he bears much fruit;
> without me you can do nothing.'
>
> (John, 15, 5)

Elizabeth told William that Tom Moore, the fellow he'd helped chop greenery with out by Bird's Close, was excellent at wood carving and could do with the work.

The Puritan taste for simplicity had meant there was no interest in his craftsmanship.

The visit to Beaumanor had been well worth it. As Spring turned into summer the fledgling hedgerows began to thrive. The scent of thyme blended with the sweetness of roses. Raspberries and strawberries took a bit more coaxing, but Elizabeth was looking forward to snatching a treat or two as soon as the fruit appeared. The Head Gardener at Beaumanor had promised to graft some fruit varieties for William, and gave him guidance on their cultivation: damsons, gages, plums, and cherries to augment their established apples and pears. All would be splendid, so long as the country could adapt to a new way of being governed. A little stability would let business thrive and ordinary citizens hope for an improvement in the quality of their lives.

William had been preoccupied with his project and had paid only scant attention to the atmosphere in the kitchen. Betty caught him alone late one afternoon to have a serious word. 'Have you been sparing a thought or two for Molly lately?' He couldn't say he had, just exchanged the usual pleasantries. She seemed her usual self, perhaps a bit quieter. 'Oh, she's quiet alright,' Betty snapped, 'trying her hardest not to break into tears, if you ask me.'

'What are you saying, Betty?'

'Well, you'd no way of knowing, it's women's business, but she's lost a bairn,'

'I didn't know, didn't notice. Ben never said a word'.

'Well he wouldn't. That's the problem. The poor wee thing was no bigger than a kitten, a perfect little handful, a

41

lad she said, months before time. They hadn't told anyone in case this was another false hope.'

'So that's why she's been away. You said her mother was ill. What do you want? Molly wouldn't want me…'

'No, not Molly, Ben. Ben won't talk about it. Won't look at her. He was counting on a son to help with the mill. Years they've been hoping. He's not right. Molly and I can have a good old cry together, we'll get through. Ben needs someone won't think less of him for being in pieces, and that's only you as far as I can see.'

'I've been blind to all this, I'm sorry, Betty. I'll do what I can.'

'Molly says he's been stopping most nights late at the Angel, so she'll be asleep when he gets home, so that's where to find him.'

William headed towards town. He wasn't sure he was the right man for the job, but no one else was queueing up for it. He suspected Ben would be tight-lipped and sullen in his cups. He prayed for guidance. The pub wasn't the right place to talk about such things. He'd need to get him alone, perhaps on the walk home.

A lad came running up the turnpike from town. 'What's the hurry, lad? Is there a fire?'

'No… no fire,' he gasped for breath, ' it's the miller's son… hurt bad. I'm sent to the Big House … fetch his missus.'

' Ben? Where is he? Where is he?'

'At the baker's, Johnson's… making a delivery. They've put him on his cart, heading back this way…' The boy was half away to the Hall and shouting back as he tore off down the road.

William quickened his pace, hoping to meet the cart as soon as it appeared. Light held on longer these summer evenings, so it should be easier to spot. Ben must have been nearing the end of his round by this time of day. The weather had been fine lately, no lashing rain, no muddy ruts, what accident had befallen him? A broken axle? A loose wheel? A spooked horse?

The cart came in sight, and he could hear the steady clopping of a horse pulling its load gently. Ben was stretched out moaning in the back, with his head heavily bandaged, soaked through with blood. One leg was at a queasy angle.

Hal Johnson pulled on the reins to halt their progress, saying they'd best not stop as Molly'd need to see him before…

'Before he gets any worse,' filled in William, not sure whether Ben was conscious enough to overhear.

'Exactly so,' nodded Hal, understanding William's caution.

'What happened? Ben's the strongest man I know. The cart, the horse are unhurt, how did this happen?'

'Have you seen his leg? It just gave way. Those sacks he hefts are near as dammit a hundredweight apiece, and shoulder height when stood on end.'

'Aye, I've seen him drop them off at the Hall., They're massive. Should take two men to shift them.'

'Well, his knee popped, the leg gave way when he had the last one across his shoulders. He'd been all hunched over, taking the strain, ready to come up the path to the door, and let out an unholy scream. Down he fell, forward

43

like. The sack and all, crushing him. We got it off him, quick as we could, but…well, you can see…we've got to hurry.'

William nodded, he walked beside the cart, reaching in to hold Ben's hand. He heard a few garbled words and told Ben he was going to stay with him. He made the sign of the cross on his forehead and felt Ben squeeze his hand. He didn't care if Sam overheard him, and started to pray with his friend, the prayers for those facing death. Ben's mumbling became more indistinct, and then there was only silence.

While he thought Ben might still hear him, he began with the twenty-second psalm, *'The Lord is my shepherd; there is nothing I shall want…'* then the consoling hundred and second psalm,

The Lord is compassion and love,
slow to anger and rich in mercy.
He does not treat us according to our sins
nor repay us according to our faults…

Ben's hand was still warm when Molly reached him. William wished the damaged head had not looked so lurid. This would be an image she could not forget. It was over. No one was at fault, there was no one to blame. He hadn't been drinking. It was an ordinary day, doing his ordinary job. Molly was a widow at twenty-nine with a seven year old daughter to raise and a cottage she owed rent on.

They held a simple funeral up in the chapel. According

44

to the law, all burials had to be conducted by the Church of England, but he was buried in a family plot by the mill. Friends gathered at the cottage to keep Molly company and share their memories. The Byerleys were not expected to come, but had Betty send over a decent ham and a keg of beer., with a basket of fresh baked bread. William was also sent over with a letter from the master to assure Molly she had her cottage for life, and she could take as much time as she needed before she returned to the Hall. Molly was smiling through her tears at the relief of not losing her home, but knew full well that 'as long as she needed' meant two days off at most.

The stories flowed, Ben as a cheeky lad, Ben the lad all the girls fancied, Ben besotted with Molly. William listened, taking in the background of the man who had befriended him. He didn't know about the men from Belgrave, Ben included, along with Tom Moore the woodsman, Samson the blacksmith and half a dozen others, who had banded together after the fighting in Leicester subsided. They packed up tools, buckets and shovels. They weren't sure if they'd be doing repairs, putting out fires or digging graves. Perhaps all three. Molly had torn sheets into bandages, and packed up a small mountain of cheese cobs. Molly wanted to join them but back then she was 'great -bellied'. No time to take risks.

Tom took up the story, 'Ben heard shouts from one tumbled down wreck. He found a man, looked in his forties, plainly dressed like a Puritan, pinned under a fallen beam. His son, maybe six or seven was with him. The boy's ankle was caught, but otherwise seemed in less distress than the father. It would take more than even Ben to free them. He called us over. A fair bit of rubble had to be cleared first to access the beam. Every judder of the beam was agony for the man, Richard, Richard Vann, a cobbler.'

'Yeah, the lad was John,' Samson continued, 'Every time the poor man shouted in pain, he tried to tell his son he was going to be fine, they were both going to be fine. I remember Ben cradling the fellow's head in his arms, giving him sips of water. It took two hours to get them out.'

'What happened to them? Did you bring them over to the hospital?'

'That would've been perfect in normal times, but it were overflowing. Ben said to pack them into the cart and take them back to Belgrave. If he couldn't persuade the Byerleys to take them in, then they'd squeeze them into their cottage somehow. He reckoned father and son shouldn't be split up; one'd help the other to recover.'

'That was quite a risk, caring for Puritans under your own roof. I've heard their rants against popery. What was he thinking? I can't see the Byerleys being comfortable with that.'

Tom laughed, 'Well, you're right, the old man wasn't. They were torn between pity and panic, but after a bit of hemming and hawing agreed to fix up a backroom off the kitchen for the pair and look after them just until we could fix up Vann's place in town. Luckily neither patient could manage the stairs to reach the chapel. Ben even fetched them a King James Bible so they could worship together. when they started to come round from it all.'

Betty nudged Molly with a chuckle. 'That's not all that happened, is it girl?'

Molly had been very quiet, adrift in all the good memories, letting them embrace her. 'Not that night, exactly, the next day it was.'

'Aye, I watched the lass waiting on the invalids, plumping up their bedding, finding them fresh clothes, washing and mending their tattered things…too much bending, too much, she shook her head, well then…'

'Then you caught me standing up against the wall, leaning into it. Resting I was. Or later rubbing my back. It wouldn't stop aching.'

'Yeah, you said it was sorting out those straw mattresses, down on all fours fixing their bedding. I knew better. When you slumped down at the kitchen table, with your head on your hands, leaning over to ease that belly, I knew.'

Molly smiled, and explained to William, 'Betty sent a lad off to fetch Ben, then walked me slow and gentle down to the cottage. The midwife said I was on the way, Betty was right.'

Tom laughed, 'That lad ran all over town trying to find the Belgrave band who were patching up shops and homes. He kept missing us. We got tired and thirsty, stopped for a pint or two after a good day's work. It was a hot day. We were filthy, sweat, soot, sawdust, downright mucky.'

'And I swear it was Ben's idea to take a dip in the Soar to cool off, clean up.'

'Sounds like him, right enough,' quipped William.

'So when the lad did find us we were dripping wet and a tad puddle-headed.'

47

'Never saw Ben run so fast in all my life! When your Becca was born he was giddy with joy, couldn't stop telling me about her tiny hands, her dainty feet, the miracle of her, like she was the first baby ever born.' Molly nodded, stroking the head of her daughter asleep on her knee.

William felt odd and uncomfortable heading down to the Angel without Ben, but he was drawn to see how his social world beyond the village was coping with his sudden loss. The room quietened when he entered, he nodded to thank them and slipped into his place beside Jake. 'Doesn't seem quite so lively without him,' was all he could think to say.

Rosie offered him a free drink. 'Play us one of your ballads, will ya? Something slow and gentle.' She found it hard to finish her request. He returned to his corner and did as she asked. No one dared speak. William looked at Jake and shook his head, 'The Ben I knew loved life, he was never solemn. Let's raise a glass to a fine good man!'

The tankards clinked, they cheered his toast and relaxed. Jake started up a lively tune and the pub felt at ease. Laughter and banter resumed. Under the multitude of voices, Jake leaned over to William, 'You did the right thing, you know. Just right. He was quite a character down here, lively like. He'll be missed.'

'I could see that. Rosie looked so upset, she could hardly speak to ask me to play.'

'Ah, well there's history there. He had an eye for the ladies did Ben,' whispered Jake.

'Sure that's no secret, Jake. ' He'd wink at anything in a skirt, he would.'

'See that pot boy over yonder? Look familiar?' The lad was sturdy, with a mop of dark curly hair. William guessed maybe eight or nine. 'That's Rosie's boy. She fancied George, the landlord's son, a gentle sort, not forthcoming with the ladies, but a promising meal ticket if you get my meaning. Rosie egged on Ben's joshing to make George jealous I reckon. He took the bait. They were quickly wed. Her skirts were riding high, they say, a little too soon. I didn't take any notice, myself. Just so's you know, like, to be careful what you say.'

'If that's true, that'd be before Molly, wouldn't it?'

'Before they were wed, leastwise. Hell, the boy might be the image of her dear departed grandad for all I know, but that's not what the old wives'll tell you.'

'Does Molly know?'

'No idea, but Ben couldn't keep his eyes off the lad. Rosie used to watch, hoping I guess that Molly would sprout a gaggle of little Bens to take his mind off her boy. You see a lot just sitting in this corner…'

1661

DEATH, THE UNINVITED GUEST

As for man, his days are like grass;
he flowers like the flower of the field;
the wind blows and he is gone
and his place never sees him again.

(Ps. 102)

William's garden design was coming into its own. The hedges were filling out and needed trimming. He made a sketch of the shears he needed and had to get the village blacksmith, christened Samuel but known as Samson, to make him a pair. It was an unusual request, as only the grander houses had acquired a taste for hedges. When he had returned to Beaumanor to collect his new fruit trees, they'd told him they'd had three hundred children turn up early at their door, singing, or more often, shouting the required jingle, begging for their Valentine buns. Molly would be amazed; she kept bragging they baked a hundred each year and they'd all disappear before nine a.m.

That happy gaggle of children bursting into the grounds of the Hall was a rare touch of jollity, one sorely needed. William Byerley had died just months after seeing his daughter wed to Humphrey Wharton and head off to London. Perhaps it was the effort of hosting them, sorting the dowry, or just the fact that his bloated body could no longer manage the stairs up to the garret chapel without stopping to rest, that he was so often out of breath. Elizabeth had been wringing her hands more than usual, fretting over his declining health, feeling helpless. She insisted he partake of medicinal cordials for his heart. One night at dinner he seemed to be listening to her and the priest, the pair of them wrapped up in how to set out the fruit trees, arriving in the Spring. When they turned to him for a response there was nothing. Nothing. Eyes open with the light gone out.

He was only fifty-six. Elizabeth was forty-nine. She fell apart, veering from uncontrollable tears to a frozen sleep-walking state, cut off from everything and everyone around her. Poor Charles, not yet twenty, was left to handle the funeral and assume responsibility for the business. He found the cleric a mature and wise head to steer him through those first difficult weeks. As for his own position, the priest felt it was only proper to request a transfer from his provincial, as it was the father, William Byerley, who had extended the invitation to shelter him, and he should not presume to expect the same from the next generation. Once the household had settled from the shock of its sudden grief, he spoke to Charles about leaving.

'On no account,' was Charles' immediate response,' you are the beating heart of this house, and its conscience. It would dishonour my father's memory were I to let you go,' a smile crossed his face, ...'and my mother would never forgive me!'

More seriously, Charles expressed his concern for the fragility of his mother. She needed the presence of the priest to calm her, by maintaining the familiar routine. 'Any priest could do that', interjected Bentney. 'True, but you are her link to Father. I know you only knew him for just over a year, but you're the only one he let share his fishing tackle...he wouldn't even let me near it! You've become part of the family, not just a chaplain. She'd fall apart without a priest here, I know that, and without you specifically, someone she can share memories with. But,' he paused, 'I need you here too. Just like in our philosophy sessions, I need someone to question my ideas, I need a grey head at the table. Running this place, trying to sound confident in business dealings... It takes years to learn these skills. Please stay.'

How could he refuse? His covert flock was grateful the new young master was carrying on as before. Father William's mission could continue: clandestine Masses, baptisms, weddings and funerals, forgiving sins, consoling the dying. His annual reports to his provincial showed a steady rise in numbers, down to births more than conversions. It was risky to convert. One young man, a student of Cambridge University, son of a Protestant minister, was converted by reading the *Ten Reasons* by Fr. Edmund Campion. Having found access to a priest, he was instructed by him and received into the Church. He told his mother what he had done, and persuaded her to speak to the same priest. He visited them at their home. The

52

father of the young man discovered what was happening and was furious. He put his wife into strict confinement in their house. She became seriously ill, on the point of death. A priest was smuggled to her bedside and she was able to receive the sacraments before she died. The son had to escape abroad to finish his studies in a Catholic college. Edward Turner, the son, followed his father into ministry, only as a Catholic priest instead.

Another priest converted some Protstants living near the house in which he was harboured. These conversions aroused the indignation of the Protestant Earl who lived nearby. He ordered a number of constables suddenly to enter the house at which the priest lived, at an early hour in the morning, in search of him. The priest was not there. After he had said Mass, he had gone out for a walk in the country. This was very unusual for him, and was observed with some surprise by the servants. Soon thereafter, the officers arrived and searched every part of the house. The priest, having finished his walk, was returning home when a Protestant peasant strongly advised him to hide in the neighbouring woods. He didn't need to be told twice, and escaped. He was moved by his superior to another part of the country where he was unknown.

Unfortunately, this escape enraged the Earl. He needed to find a scapegoat to assuage his frustration and apprehended a known Catholic who had befriended the priest. The man was thrown into prison and 'after great sufferings' died there.

There was no consistency in how these matters were treated, which made it all the more terrifying. One priest was apprehended as he was visiting the homes of Catholics by night, in order to administer the sacraments. The officers intended to take him before a magistrate, but because the nearest one lived many miles away, they felt 'some consideration' for the old man that was their prisoner. They accepted a sum of money, call it a bribe or an instant fine, and released him. The 'consideration' seemed to have worked both ways.

There were about ten priests working in the Leicester/ Derby district at any one time, covering a vast area and usually sheltered by better-off families. The Franciscan who was working in Leicester, Thomas Smith, tended to stay in the town administering to the less affluent, dropping in at Belgrave from time to time. Father William found a selection of Franciscan books left there for safe-keeping. Father Thomas was not well provided for, serving the poor with little financial backing. There were reports reaching the Hall that he was seen selling vegetables near the market, trying to raise a pittance to subsist on. Molly thought perhaps Father William could track him down and bring him a basket of provisions and an invite for a short stay to feed him up and give him a well-earned rest from his hardships. The pair of them reckoned what with young Mr. Byerley having to deal with so much, the Belgrave household had let slip the plight of the Franciscan on their doorstep.

Becca was now a competent cook, an assistant to her mother. At sixteen she was lovely as a rosebud, not quite in full bloom but showing all the promise. Betty decided she'd had enough. Molly had had a word with the Mistress

Elizabeth, to persuade Betty that she had earned her rest. It was all part of a devious women's plot: Old Ted was the groundsman at the Hall; he too should be stepping down as his joints were so stiff that his gardening was both very slow and painful. Father William was hoping Mr. Byerley would take on the blacksmith's boy, Tom, instead, someone the gardener-priest could train up. Ted had a cottage in the village, but living alone, he preferred to stop in Betty's kitchen for most of his meals.

For decades the pair had been teasing each other, tossing out barbs to see if one could outdo the other. It was obvious they cared for one another. Neither would make a move, probably neither dared. It's a vulnerable business not being in the flush of youth, risking rejection. Mrs. Byerley was told what was planned, but her efforts were held in reserve in case their first plan failed. William was to speak with Ted, Molly with Betty. Molly was simply practical: you need to lighten the load, find a place to live…wouldn't cooking for two be pleasanter than the hassle of the Great House? You've been feeding him longer than most folk have been married, why not make it official? Father William was more about the heart: you know she loves you ('she has a peculiar way of showing it'), you know you've had an eye for her for as far back as anyone can remember('no fool like an old fool'), wouldn't it be nice to have her fixing those pies and stews just for you, sitting with you each night by the fire snug in your own cottage?('she'd never agree to that') What if I said she might?

They only needed a nudge; it was what they both had

hoped. Their banter took on a bit of shyness once the engagement was announced. Molly swore she even saw Betty blush.

Their nuptials might have been the trigger to set Mrs. Byerley's mind abuzz about finding a suitable bride for Charles. Christmas festivities were prime match-making opportunities. For several seasons the young Master claimed he wasn't interested. Then the woman was too young, too old, too silly. Too grand to consider him, too poor to bring him any status. His mother's fussing was beginning to annoy him. The only way to defuse this attention was to find someone, a wife, lady of the manor. His mother, the dowager, the widow, would be left to her prayers and her good works, on the periphery.

He married Mary, daughter and sole heir of Samuel Cuttler of Ipswitch, to whom he was introduced by a fellow merchant. She was several years older than Charles, but not noticably, and well educated. Father William thought she'd be a great, steadying influence on the young man and perhaps the thought of a houseful of grandchildren would enliven Mistress Elizabeth.

Much to everyone's delight the new Mrs. Byerley was quickly expecting their first child. A daughter, named Elizabeth after her grandmother, was born in 1659. The following year was a momentous time for the country. The brief experiment under Cromwell's Commonwealth was over. His son Richard had tried to carry on the project but proved a disaster, nicknamed Tumble-Down Dick. 1660 saw the Restoration of the monarchy with Charles II on the throne.

In Belgrave Hall, the Byerleys celebrated the birth of a son, Joseph. Mistress Mary seemed to thrive on childbearing. She declined the services of a wet nurse, revelling in precious hours spent in the nursery. It was unusual for a woman of means to suckle her own children, although the Puritans recommended the practice. Mrs. Byerley did not like the slatternly looks of the women who offered themselves for the service, and she had heard too many tales of babies smothered by their nurses 'over-laying' the infant as they slept. The wet-nurses' own children did not look robust enough to suggest this was a healthy choice. Handbooks suggested that a nurse's complexion was an indicator of the quality of her milk. Red hair and freckles, apparently, were dangerous because they signified sour milk. Brown hair was preferred. Having begun her child-bearing somewhat later than others of her social standing, Mistress Mary preferred to be cautious and didn't mind if others thought her 'unusual.'

Little Elizabeth was two in the Spring of 1661. A lively child, keen to run free and exhaust her nanny. The child had rosy plump cheeks and an infectious giggle that delighted her grandmother. After her afternoon nap, the two Elizabeths would stroll around the garden, the grandmother trying to keep up with the toddler's headlong rush along the winding paths. She was beginning to learn her colours pointing at the blooms, 'lellow' and 'burble', pointing at the crocuses.

Mary would normally rest in the afternoons, usually with Joseph in her arms. The two women had markedly different personalities. The new Mrs. Byerley was far more out-going, warmer and more relaxed. Mistress Elizabeth had always been more reserved, and largely kept to herself and her charitable visits, except for this brief private time with the child, when no one could observe her enjoying that simple indulgence.

Perhaps it was the grandmother's good works that brought the trouble to the Hall. Perhaps it was one of the servants. Scarlet fever. There was no cure. The two Elizabeths were struck down, burning up. They kept them in separate rooms to give them each a better chance of recovery. Mrs. Byerley was told she must not risk comforting her daughter for fear of spreading the illness to her son. She ordered they both be treated with tinctures of Gascon's Powder. This came highly recommended by the Countess of Kent, 'These and many other Experiments have I with good success tryed, and with God's blessing recovered diverse patients.' Gascon's Powder was used to treat smallpox, measles, spotted or purple fever, for 'swoonings of the heart from malignant vapours' or even against the Plague or Pestilent Fevers. It was a way of doing something, offering hope, something beyond mopping a sweaty brow or changing soaked bed linen. Grandmother and granddaughter died within hours of each other on March 4th.

Naturally Mr. Byerley sent word to his sister Anne in London. It would be impossible for her to return in time for the double funeral, but he hoped she could return to pay her respects when it could be arranged. Anne replied with a great outpouring of sympathy for her brother and his wife, and assured them her priest would be saying Masses for the repose of the soul of her mother. The dear child, an innocent, would have been welcomed straight into the arms of her merciful Creator. Correspondence had been very infrequent since her marriage. Excuses had been made as to why the couple could not visit over the twelve days of Christmas. The elder Elizabeth had assumed hopefully that it was because Anne might be in a 'delicate' state of health, and had longed for news of another grandchild. No such news had been forthcoming.

They waited months to hear when Anne might visit. A brief letter finally arrived in July. Humphrey had died suddenly during Easter week.

The doctor said it was the 'Bloody flux'. He had recently returned from a voyage to the Low Countries to secure a contract, and had been unwell for days afterward. It is common on ships, the doctor told me. Usually the officers and more prosperous passengers eat better and avoid it. Apparently quite a number from all levels were taken ill. He was fifty-six, so he lived to a fair age.

It has been a difficult time. His children by his first marriage are of course in deepest mourning, but I suspect there is also an element of great deliverance. They never accepted me, although their father insisted they welcome me. They watched me constantly for any sign of a step-rival. Humphrey was a kind man, gentle, but not keen to antagonise his grown family. The several times I miscarried, for all his soothing words, I could tell he was greatly relieved. It is hard to grieve for a child on one's own.

He appreciated our companionship, but I began to feel that his choice to remarry was one he grew to regret.

I was never in fact the true lady of the household. Everything ran as it always had. His sons and their wives ignored me. I was no better than a despised mistress. There was never any consideration given to the notion that we might join you for Christmas. Only the London world mattered.

I hate the city. It is an unhealthy place. I long to return to Leicester, its broad rolling hills and clean air. I long to wander round Father William's garden, nibbling on strawberries or plucking raspberries, waiting for his fruit trees to hang heavy.

Our Father died too soon. Father would have protested on my behalf, but after his death, Humphrey changed his will to safeguard his older children's inheritance. As soon as he thought I might be with child, his sons confronted him. To allay their fears he transferred his property and business interests into his sons' names. I have been left my widow's third but it is a third of the dregs. The will requests them to accomodate his widow, but to remain under their unwilling sufferance would be intolerable.

I beg you, dear brother, please make room for me. Let me come home and leave this sorrowful, unloving abode.

Mr. Byerley immediately sent for Anne. The Whartons, delighted to be rid of their unwanted step-mother, packed her off in style, letting her use the family's carriage and four horses, so long as it was promptly returned. Anne had made a timely choice, albeit brought about by her husband's demise. London was an unhealthy city. Within four years the capital would be struck down by plague. Rich merchants fled the city with their families. Not one in a hundred was left. When news of the epidemic reached Belgrave, Anne wondered if the Whartons had escaped. In the following year, when the Great Fire spread across the City, she wondered if anything was left of the life she once knew.

Leicester was familiar with plague. Every ten years or so a particularly virulent outbreak cut off communication with London. It stopped the fairs and even local trade was severely hampered. Charles had watched his father deal with such crises; he calmed fears, telling his warehousemen that their wages were secure, that things would pick up when the pestilence had moved on. Privately he watched his savings dwindle, wondering how long it would take.

Mrs. Byerley had to wean Joseph when her daughter died; the milk wouldn't come in her distress. Losing the comfort of suckling her boy caused the woman even more heartache. She seemed always on the verge of tears. She wearily agreed to her sister-in-law joining the household; Anne was in an impossible situation and of course she must come, but Mary barely knew her. She wasn't sure she had the energy to forge a sisterly bond with a stranger.

Anne kept to herself initially, taking long walks,

reading in the summer house, listening to the music of this house, getting a feel for the tempo. It would take a good listener to find how she might fit in. Father William saw her at Mass each morning. The whole family were dressed in sombre shades, mourning both Elizabeths and Humphrey. Mistress Anne was devout, but not as pious as her mother.

Several of the widow's trunks contained books, hidden between her dresses. The family had been so focused on Anne not spiriting away valuable jewellery, the family silver or their Venetian glassware, that they were not concerned when each evening she slipped into Humphrey's study to fetch a bit of bedtime reading. A love of reading was something she and Humphrey had shared, but not an interest inherited by his sons. They failed to notice that none of these splendid leather-bound volumes was ever returned. When the servants reported to them that Anne was ordering her maidservant, that girl she brought from Belgrave, to pack all her clothes, they were delighted. They had won, forced her to flee London.

Mistress Anne may not have returned with a generous settlement, but she had her own small library. Education for his daughter had not been a priority for William Byerley. He was not alone. Most thought only boys needed anything more than rudimentary literacy and numeracy. Even the Jesuits. Anne found a freedom in this new-found widowhood to rectify that.

Father William hoped Anne might confide in him about her difficult marriage. She seemed so alone, with the master and his wife distracted by their double bereavement.

The priest did not want to be a distant retainer, simply kept on to administer sacraments when required. It took some time for her to accept his friendship. She was wary of his opinion of the role of women. He probably thought she should remarry and produce a 'quiverful' of offspring, or remain a grieving widow, honouring the memory of her late husband. Neither role appealed to her.

She was ready to lambast him with the practicalities of her situation. She was no longer young, had no substantial fortune to attract suitors, and with a history of miscarriages was not likely to provide any suitable heirs. For any man seeking a first wife, she was not a good bet. As for the role of a second wife to a widower, she was determined never to be in that unenviable position again. Had Humphrey not had grown children, she might well have looked forward to growing in love with him. She had so little time with him alone. His children always came first, always had his full attention. It wasn't enough, not nearly enough. She'd wear her widowhood as a badge of honour earned, but not in any crippling grief.

'Is there no room for the chance of love?' Father William gently suggested.

'Never likely, but never discounted. It isn't in a woman's gift to seek it, she must be sought, so it is better to craft a life without such expectations, than waste it in fruitless hope,' Mistress Anne reflected.

'So what will you do? With no disrespect, I don't see you satified with hours in the chapel or concentrating on your needlework. Helping out Mary with her charitable efforts, perhaps?'

'If it will help keep the peace, fine, but as you suggest I want a more active course. My father's attitude towards women and their right to an education cannot be allowed to continue to hamper us in this generation. The Puritans at least have the ideal of equality in our access to learning.'

'They've not done much to support it though, have they? And as for Catholics being educated, well, we tried in Derby to set up a few small classes back before the war. They were discovered and shut down when we'd thought the atmosphere was more tolerant.'

'There's a boarding school for girls being set up in Leicester, did you know?'

'No, it won't be admitting papists, so no one has mentioned it to me. Only the richest, I presume, could afford it. How does that help your cause? What are they offering, lute playing and French lessons to catch a rich husband?'

'I haven't surveyed the curriculum, but perhaps it doesn't include Latin or the classics. It's a start. Wasn't it Thomas More who wrote that a wife should be 'learned if possible, or at least capable of being so' ?

'Ah, yes, but that was last century. Our enlightened sovereign, James, did you no great service. He refused to have his daughter taught Latin, remember, because he thought 'to make women learned and foxes tame had the same effect: to make them more cunning'.

'Well if all he had to go on was the silliness of his daft Queen Anne, I can understand why he might think that, but there are better examples. I heard stories about Mary Ward, a nun hiding in 'plain clothes' which were actually the height of fashion to invite young ladies to her London open houses. She managed to escape the notice of government informers. Lots of families sent their girls over to the Low Countries to get educated, Knatchbulls, Gages, Vavasours, Blundells.'

'Yes, but she was a bit headstrong, getting into trouble with church authorities back on the continent. Not a perfect role model, Mrs. Wharton.'

'I grant you she ran into difficulties, and that many of her pupils chose to stay abroad and become nuns. That is not a solution.'

'I want to find a way to maintain my freedom, stay in England, keep my faith and pursue an education for myself and other like-minded women, and not just affluent ones.'

'That's a fine and laudable ambition, dear Mistress Anne, but a tricky one to achieve. If you cause too much of a stir, the authorities will be forced to look at this household more closely, endangering all of us, and all those who attend Mass up in the chapel or those to whom I bring the sacraments in their homes. It only takes one suspected member of our community to be pressured into giving testimony against us all.'

'Obviously, your danger would be greater than anyone else's. You don't have to remind me. My brother would be tried for harbouring you, and our whole world could unravel…but there must be something I can do, something that wouldn't arouse suspicion?'

'I have heard that some educated ladies take it upon themselves to teach their staff, and some even see it as an act of charity to teach the village children and buy them books. Not setting up a formal school to draw any official attention, but seen as training to better their prospects in life. Simply good management, one could say. Not likely to upset anyone's applecart…'

'And if those few grow to value my efforts, and maybe wish their children have the same chance, who's to say where it might lead? Small steps it is, then. A worthy occupation for the widowed aunt, and something Mistress Mary would approve, I'm sure. Once the children are older, she might even join me in my efforts. Maybe it could do some good. Not change the world, just one village.'

'One village, I think you'll find, will entail a great deal of planning and effort. You have the enthusiasm, the intelligence, and , I might add, the charm, to persuade any number of staff to be your willing pupils.They'll tell you dutifully they want to be able to read the Bible, but never forget how many hours they work, how bone-weary they are. Give them some light relief, a ballad to giggle over, maybe a bit of poetry. The 'Song of Songs' is Biblical, but frank enough to keep them interested. My pupils had no choice but to study whatever I chose; yours will need to be enticed. You'll have to hook them in, snatching whatever fleeting free time they're allowed. If you can manage that, you'll prove a better teacher than I'll ever be.'

Father William held her hand and wished her well with her plan, offering to support her with practical advice and as mentor. Mistress Anne, he felt, would thrive with a sense of purpose, and hoped the Byerleys would welcome her efforts.

1678

THE POPISH PLOT

I trusted, even when I said:
'I am sorely afflicted,'
and when I said in my alarm:
'No man can be trusted.'

(Ps. 115)

Mistress Anne very much enjoyed her chosen task, finding that delight in learning and teaching which meant that she could not discern which endeavour could be described as work or leisure. She had developed a correspondence with another educated woman of her generation, Nancy Denton, whose father, Dr. Denton, had insisted she be educated in the classics. They shared a dislike of the fashion for teaching prosperous middle class girls only dainty French and a few musical accomplishments, while impoverished girls were expected to focus on needlework, with little emphasis on literacy. Anne wrote to Nancy about Leicester's new girls' boarding school, only for the better off, of course, but with the understanding that girls 'had a natural weakness'. Had Anne the financial backing and had she not been a Catholic, doubtless she and Nancy might have set up an inspiring institution, but Anne had to work in the modest sphere of Belgrave.

Father William had other pastoral duties, beyond his small chapel congregation. Franciscan priests had been using Belgrave as a base long before his own arrival. He'd been friends with Father Thomas Smith for years, worrying about his hardships looking after the poorer faithful in the town. Father Thomas had come to stay over the Christmas holidays in 1666, and subsequently it was clear he had only weeks to live. The Byerleys treated him like an honoured member of the family, kept him wrapped up by the fire, with Becca fixing him warm broth and coaxing him with savoury treats. While he was strong enough, he could celebrate Mass, but once he retired to his sickbed, Holy Communion was brought to him as long as he was conscious. The last saccrament, the anointing, Extreme Unction, and the Viaticum(the last Communion) were administered before Father Thomas slipped into his final sleep. It was a peaceful end, surrounded by those who had known and cared for him for years. A good death.

William envied him. Father Thomas had chosen a tougher path and seen it through. The Byerley's chaplain had lived in comparative luxury in Belgrave Hall, serving a limited flock in a well appointed chapel. He had drifted through his vocation, neither serving the destitute like this poor Franciscan, nor influencing the powerful, like some of his fellow Jesuits. In dangerous times, he'd had a cosy life, tutoring a few children, tinkering with a bit of garden design. Not exactly heroic. Nothing to boast about to his Father Provincial. No dramatic conversions to speak of.

An entirely forgettable life. A disappointment to the Order no doubt.

It was ten years before another Franciscan came to stay at the Hall, Father Gervase Cartwright. He would be the last Franciscan to stay with the Byerleys, and would come to play an important role in Father William's life. Perhaps his low key missionary work in Leicester was not seen as a disappointment in the eyes of the Byerleys; after William Bentney it was only Jesuits they would request as chaplains. Perhaps, as events transpired, they felt they owed it to his memory.

Father William was sixty-nine. Father Gervase had been in Leicester for a year and seemed to have settled. He chose to serve the poor in town as had his predecessor, but to live, albeit simply, at the Hall. He would never dine with the family and was almost invisible around the place. He did, however, concede that joining William for a spot of river fishing now and again was in keeping with his self-imposed austerity. William was grateful for clerical company. He was required to report to his Provincial in Derbyshire and make provision for his own regular confession, but that was a formal interaction. It had been a very long time since he had been able to speak freely, even if Father Gervase was young enough to be his son. Gervase was also a great reader, and another reason he preferred the Hall to living in town was that it was a safe place to keep his books.

Father William's tutoring days were coming to a close. Joseph was eighteen and was never scholastically minded. He and the priest were not best suited, a clash of personalities from the outset. The younger brother, named Charles after his father, was fourteen, still quite boyish, and happy to be delving into the classics for the sheer mental exercise it demanded. Joseph, however, was consumed by the heady thrill of being the eldest son, destined to inherit the Hall, the business, the whole aura of being master of all he surveyed. He thought his father was far too unadventurous, too timid to try and expand their enterprise, too uninterested in flattering the right people to smooth the way. Joseph had an eye for fashion, wanting his parents to dress with the right flair, serve more elaborate food at social gatherings. They didn't seem to have the knack of impressing their guests, enteraining them warmly, certainly, but impressing them? Not in Joseph's eyes.

Father William had another reason to find Joseph a problem. He had a rather dismissive attitude towards the servants which ran counter to the general kindliness of the Byerley household. Mistress Anne had asked the priest for advice about one of the staff she was teaching. Joseph was pestering her, threatening her with dismissal if she refused him. The girl was terrified, ruined if she complied, dismissed if she didn't. She feared next time he got hold of her alone, she wouldn't be given a choice. Anne made sure the girls worked in pairs whenever he was about.

Father William had a word with Mr. Byerley, who initially tried to make light of the incident, that all young men try their luck with a comely lass, then with a glower from his chaplain, thought better of it. A young woman's virtue should not be in danger in a respectable household, the reputation of his family, the role the Hall played in the community...it began to sink in. Joseph was called in and given a thorough dressing down, and Mr. Byerley threatened to disinherit him if any such disgrace should occur as a result of his actions. Joseph bowed his head and submitted to his father's tirade, but flashed unremitting hatred at the old priest as he left the room, convinced it was he who had brought this backstairs business to his father's attention.

Father William understood all too well the nature of that look. He had no wish to be still at Belgrave Hall when that young man became its master, and he was quite sure the feeling was mutual. Perhaps he could retire from the active mission at seventy, return to the Continent, perhaps teach at St. Omer's. Perhaps Mr. Byerley might write to his superiors, suggest a younger man replaces him. This posting was getting decidedly uncomfortable.

Although neither he nor Mistress Anne had said anything, the servants all knew what had happened. Mr. Byerley, of course, told his wife. Joseph had gone out to the stables, had his horse saddled up and tore off. Everyone was relieved he was gone, expected he'd get drunk somewhere and not return till daybreak. Charles decided it was best if the boy went away for awhile, give things a chance to calm down. Mary suggested a visit to her cousins, the Beaumonts, out at the village of Gracedieu. It seemed the perfect solution.

The family may have tried to engineer a bit of peace, but national events conspired against them. Six years earlier Charles II had issued the Declaration of Indugence, which allowed Catholics the right to worship in private houses. Dissenters had to apply for a license for this privilege. Although it was meant as a measure to strengthen the security of the state, it did nothing to allay suspicions. It was seen as a sell-out to the Catholic threat from France. The King was being bankrolled by the French and a return to the 'tyranny' of Catholicism was feared.

Lord Danby, the self-styled Voice of the Shires, was a fierce Anglican, and leader of the new administration. His government rescinded the Declation of Indulgence, putting in its place an anti-Catholic Test Act, requiring all public office holders to take an oath to deny the Catholic doctrine of transubstaniation and to conform to the Anglican settlement. There was growing resentment, because of his control, with little scope within Parliament for disagreement. In coffee houses, clubs, taverns and printing shops the dissent built. The twin topics were the wickedness of the Crown party and the existence of a Catholic conspiracy.

The occupants of Belgrave Hall watched the tension building and wondered how it would impact upon their lives. It had seemed so reassuring having the King restored, order, stability and a promise of a prosperous future. Now nothing felt safe or secure.

It was into this cauldron that the fake Popish Plot put forward by Titus Oates and Isreal Tonge broke, and created a maelstrom of panic. Seventeen new newspapers sprang up. There were poems, broadsides, cartoons, bawdy songs, ballads, all featuring some grotesque Catholic menace foisted on the good British public by the King. He was an easy target, with his bevy of mistresses, lavish lifestyle and his agreement with France's Louis to achieve tolerance for Catholics to secure his loans.

Oates' fantastical 'revelations' claimed that there was a plot to assassinate the King master-minded by the Jesuits, and to replace him with his brother, the Catholic James. This would establish a French-Catholic absolutist regime supported by French troops. Oates had inside knowledge of the Jesuits. He had been thrown out of two Jesuit colleges, Colegio de los Inglese Valladolid in Spain and St. Omer in France. He took very detailed notes and confided his 'spying' to a London clergyman, Isreal Tonge. Tonge was a renowned scholar but had lost his vicarage and his extensive libary to the Great Fire of London. He was eager to swallow all of Oates' claims because Tonge, like most other people, believed the Great Fire was the work of Catholic arsonists.

Titus Oates' allegations resulted in the arrest of five Catholic noblemen, Jesuit priests and lay men and women associated with them. A man-hunt went throughout the country to track down the culprits and show them no mercy. Priests were fleeing back to France, desperate to escape execution at Tyburn. Most intended to wait out the furore on the Continent, then slip back in quieter times to come. Oates accused eighty-one people. Anyone who was named on that list was in danger. Priests concocted new names to hide their identities; if they could not leave the country, at least they were trying to find safety in the hinterlands, far from major towns and cities. At least fifteen were executed, including Oliver Plunkett, the Catholic Archbishop of Armagh. Apprentice gangs were threatening violence. Crowds transformed Guy Fawkes celebrations into Pope burning on countless bonfires.

After three years opinion began to turn against Oates. The King himself had caught him out in a number of inaccuracies. The Lord Chief Justice, William Scroggs, began to declare more people innocent. Danby, who had helped promulgate Oates' allegations and perhaps helped to form the list of suspects, and his Whig party suffered a backlash.

After the election of 1678, Leicester was represented in Parliament by John Grey, who had the support of Rutland, and by Sir Henry Beaumont, who held lands at Stoughton and Thurnby. Beaumont had the reputation of being a 'thorough Royalist'. Sir Henry was part of the Anglican wing of the Beaumonts, who were therefore eligible to serve in Parliament and hold public office. The Gracedieu Beaumonts were Catholics. Sir Henry was a careful man, keen to be on the winning side at the right moment. Although his father had been created a baronet by Cromwell, Henry was happy to serve Charles II at the Restoration, especially as the king re-granted his title.

In 1679 as a Tory he was in favour of impeaching Lord Danby, but within a few years it was prudent to switch horses and go over to the Whigs. For all his manoeuvring, his one constant was a strong dislike of Catholics and resistence to their employment in public affairs. He would never vote to repeal the Test Act or any of the Penal Laws.

In the midst of this the Byerleys were having to deal with their Joseph. Mrs. Byerley contacted Gracedieu and a visit was arranged. Sir Thomas and his wife Vere had five daughters, Cicely, Vere, Jane, Mary, and Anne. The older sisters were of marriagable age and the younger would be giggly at the thought of their handsome cousin paying them any attention. Joseph hoped Sir Thomas might take him hunting to break up the non-stop chatter of the young ladies, and greatly regretted there were no male cousins in residence. He would sorely need a drinking companion.

His mother appreciated her son's view of this proposed visit, and to prevent him embarrassing the family with his moods, she relented and let him ride there on his own rather than take the carriage. He could go off for an escape from the house whenever he pleased on his own mount.

The three eldest girls were not as silly as he feared. In fact, they were rather well informed and took a keen interest in the political maelstrom that was being fanned by the sensationalist press. They showed Joseph their collection of broadsheets, cartoons and pamphlets which he'd heard about and seen a couple of the milder ones in Leicester pubs. The ferocity of the hatred and fear they were whipping up against Catholics, and Jesuits in particular, shocked the girls but Joseph read them all and said nothing.

After several weeks of gentle socialising, Sir Thomas, Mary and Jane came down with very heavy colds. The house was quiet, turned in on itself, nursing the invalids. It was not a place for guests. Joseph thanked his hostess and made his excuses. He hoped his father had calmed down and there would be no further talk of disinheriting him.

The inflamatory propaganda had given him an idea. In the empty hours while the household had fussed over its sneezing inhabitants, he had fashioned a letter to Leicester's local M.P., his Church of England cousin, Sir Henry Beaumont. One of his residences, at Stoughton Grange, was only a few miles southeast of Belgrave. Joseph was sure they would see his letter reached Sir Henry at his Westminster lodgings. The post riders were quite reliable. A letter posted on Tuesday would reach London by Friday, and a reply reach Leicester by the following Tuesday. Nothing too specific, nothing to connect to the Oates' conspiracy, but if Sir Henry was minded to make a clean sweep of the diabolical Jesuits in his constituency, he might start by seeking out Father William Bentney at Belgrave.

In the early stage of the crisis, while Oates was still believed, twenty-four victims had been hanged, drawn and quartered and hundreds imprisoned. Joseph, however, was well informed and knew that some of the more recent trials had resulted in acquittals, some men had only been arrested then let go. He wanted old Bentney to feel the fear, to be humiliated and holed up in some rat-infested stinking cell. The fright alone would probably see him off. He deserved it, 'He had no right to run off to my father and carry on as if I'd done something terrible, unforgivable. The girl was fine. She came to no harm. There was no need to make such a fuss over nothing. I did no more, and a good bit less, than any lusty youth. That old priest knows nothing of the real world. My father should have listened to me, not him.'

Beyond his personal dislike of the interfering old priest, Joseph felt trapped in his situation as the elder son, raised in a class tradition of social service and then denied any chance of following it. Even when he inherited Belgrave Hall and his father's business, there would be little he could do. He would not be allowed to affiliate with more prosperous wool merchants. He could not improve the family's prospects. He could not hold any public office, although he could plainly see how Leicester would benefit from some strategic town planning and sorting out the course of the meandering River Soar. His future would be thwarted by being labelled a dangerous member of the nation. He was made as good as useless. If he was willing now to turn in a Jesuit, and indicated he wanted to turn from Catholicism and take the Oath, when he inherited the fines would be lifted and a world of career opportunities would open for him. The womenfolk could hang on to their Popish ways and keep their tame Franciscan. Women didn't matter.

The more he thought about it, the more he was convinced that the Jesuit was the stumbling block in his life. Get rid of him and his life was full of possibilities. Let him be hunted down, put him under threat. No one could suspect the old man of seriously being a danger to anyone, let alone the the king. He'd be let go, Joseph was certain, and shipped off to the Continent, back to his masters. Out of Joseph's life for good. No doubt his father would be furious, but in the arrogance of youth, Joseph was confident he could talk his father round to the practicalities of his at least seeming to accept the national religion, especially if his father agreed to step down from managing the warehouses. It was the only logical way forward.

It was a simple enough task to ride a little beyond Belgrave to drop off the letter and sit back and wait to see if anything came of it. When he eventually returned home, the servants were curious because he seemed to arrive from the wrong direction, but were wise enough to say nothing except among themselves.

1681

THE NET TIGHTENS

A pure heart create for me, O God,
put a steadfast spirit within me.
Do not cast me away from your presence,
nor deprive me of your holy spirit.

(Ps.50)

The letter reached the Westminster lodgings as Sir Henry was dining with another midlands MP, Sir Gilbert Clarke, who represented Derbyshire. Sir Gilbert had been a Justice of the Peace for Derbyshire for many years, and a commissioner for assessment. This gave him responsibility for the Recusant Rolls in his district; he knew the better off Catholic families, those most likely to harbour secret priests.

Sir Gilbert had also been in receipt of information suggesting possible arrests. Some were clearly not worth following up, but others looked more promising. George Busby, sometimes calling himself Brown, was such a man. His neighbour, George Gilbert (also a Justice of the Peace) owned the Locko estate a few miles from the Powtrell's manor house. The Powtrells were a powerful Catholic family. It was rumoured that the owner's wife,

Anne, was the niece of George Busby who lived there as their Jesuit chaplain. He'd been in residence for six or seven years.

George Busby was born in Brussels in 1638. His family hailed from Oxfordshire but fled to the Continent because of the troubles during the Civil War. He entered the Society of Jesus at eighteen and studied at Watten. He was sent to the English Mission in 1668 to serve the Derbyshire district. On March 16, 1681 he was arrested at the Powtrell mansion and sent to Derby gaol, to await his trial for treason at the Derby Assizes in the Summer Assizes. He was forty-three. An older brother, Charles, and a cousin, John, were also Jesuit priests, but were not in England at the time of the Oates' Plot.

George Gilbert was a patient man. He'd obtained a warrant for Busby's arrest in 1678, concerned that Busby might be involved in the Plot. Busby had already fled to the Continent for safety and did not risk returning for two years. Things had been quiet in Derbyshire, so he thought it had been long enough. As soon as his neighbour was told the uncle was seen in the garden, Gilbert came to the house to buy wood for his coal-pits. When he had gained entry, he searched the house. He brought half a dozen men and sent for the constable. Mrs. Powtrell 'was in a great passion and much troubled' for fear they sought her uncle. A widow who also lived there swore he was in Flanders and that they hadn't seen him for two years.

They didn't find the man, but they found his chamber. There they confiscated a red damask vestment, an alb, a stole, an altar stone, surplice, a box of wafers and various mass books. Gilbert took these to the assizes where Justice Charlton told him they should be burnt. Gilbert had a better idea. He returned them to the Powtrells, claiming that as heirlooms, they were not important. This was a ruse to lull them into a false security.

At eleven o'clock that same night he returned and set men in the garden and in the yard to watch for any light or sound of footsteps in the loftspace. More men and the constable set about a thorough search. The widow answered in her nightclothes and made a fuss about opening the door so late, to give time for the priest to hide.

They went straight to his chamber where there had been a fire recently extinguished, some clothes were still warm and the mattress had been turned so the warmth of it was underneath. The pillow, sheets and nightcap they found hidden in the widow's chamber. In the garden men could hear someone pacing. Gilbert said he 'was resolved to find him or starve him out.' They found him in the roof space by ten o'clock the next morning. Gilbert received a £100 reward for his trouble of course.

They found a good deal of correspondence in Busby's chamber. He had contact with most of the Catholic families in Derbyshire and Leicestershire. He was a local superior it seems. 'Probably knew the man your cousin is naming,' Sir Gilbert surmised.

The Derbyshire MP drew on his pipe, 'Byerley? Byerley, you say? My first wife, Jane, was a Byerley, the Yorkshire branch. Staunch Church of England, mind you…at least you won't have to offer a reward to find him. If he's as old as the letter says, he surely can't can't outrun your men.'

'Ah, no, but getting anyone to testify against him may cost me a pretty penny, I reckon. They're a damned close bunch, but we'll see. A little sweetener usually loosens tongues to sing whatever song you please.'

'The sooner we get this wrapped up, the better, before jurys go soft on the idea. If you have any trouble finding witnesses, I have a man in Derby that will swear your man said Mass for them. He used to work for the Powtrells, says he converted to their ways to gain their trust. He was sacked for thieving and relishes telling tales. They're pretty convincing, but he'll say anything for a fat purse.'

Sir Henry easily rounded up Father William, who was carted off to Derby to join George Busby. Sir Henry's men started asking around the town and surrounding villages if anyone knew anything about this suspected priest. Could anyone swear he'd said Mass or administered any other sacraments?

The Byerleys were badly shaken that their house had been searched and that such a frail old man had been so roughly bundled away. Mr. Byerley slipped the sheriff a fair offering to treat him well; from the scowl he received in reply, it might have been money wasted. The whole household were upset, except for Joseph who watched in silence. Father William had been a fixture for decades. For nearly the past twenty years since the senior Charles had died, the priest had been a father figure to them all, at ease and jovial with the staff and wise and learned with his tutoring.

The town were equally shocked. This good, gentle man with his fiddle was no 'diabolical traitor'. He was a good listener, a wise counsellor, easy to talk to. Down at the Angel, the landlord threw out the man trying to leave his handbills, seeking anyone to act as a witness, promising it would be 'worth their while' to cooperate with Sir Henry. The burly innkeeper with his dark mane of tousled hair looked vaguely familiar. To those with a long memory, he was the image of Ben, who'd died delivering sacks of flour years ago. The inn had been transferred to the lad with splendid hair, once he had outgrown washing pots.

The landlord remembered how some twelve years back he'd found the old man down by the river the summer after his mother had died. He was not yet twenty then, full of confused thoughts, anger, grief, and the frustration of having to keep his pain buried. His only release was chucking stones into the water, not the artful sidestroke skimming to get as many bounces as he could, but violent thrusts. The loud splashes caused a shout from the fiddler who'd been quietly fishing. 'I'm not known for catching much, but you're not improving my chances any, scaring them all away!'

It wasn't meant harshly. Living up at the Big House, he hardly needed to fish for his supper. When the young man came over to apologise, Father William propped his rod by the bank and they sat under a hanging elm. It didn't take long for all the misery to come tumbling out. No one had ever told him, 'this man is a secret priest.' Saying things out loud was not safe when you weren't sure who might be listening, especially in an inn. A life spent interpreting nods and meaningful looks told the lad this man was someone he could confide in, someone he could trust.

'It's the names, you see, the names they'd gang up and call me. A boy on his own wouldn't dare. I was always big, they'd run off if I looked crossways at 'em, no, they'd wait in groups in the market to throw stones, shout 'bastard' or say horrible things about my mother'...He plucked at the grass and avoided William's eyes.

William began to understand why the lad kept to himself, never went about with young men his own age. 'Did your parents know about this?'

'My father saw it. He shooed them away a few times, and would take me out back to put a wet rag on my head if the stones had caught me. I only asked 'why?' once, and he said it was because I came early after they were wed, and I didn't look like him.' The young man's voice trailed off. He idly chucked blades of grass into the water.

Father William saw his line twitch and went to check. He needed to answer carefully. 'A lot of babies come before time,' the priest slowly, softly offered, 'and your parents were married right enough when you arrived. You're no bastard, no matter what they call you.'

'True, true, but they say I look like the miller's son, who used to be a regular at the Angel. Mother was friendly with him I hear.' He snapped a twig he'd been toying with.

'So was I,' William had his suspicions too, but had no certainty, 'It was Ben who first brought me to your pub. Your mum was friendly with all of us, it was her job to be jolly and joke and keep us supping up. I never saw anything else.' He had not lied. ' Who did your mother say you took after?'

'She said I was the image of her grandfather, who

84

was quite handily long dead. I'm not sure I believed her. We never spoke of it again. I'll never know.' The youth slumped in misery against the tree, gouging the earth with his heel.

The priest let the silence sit between them. He busied himself re-baiting his hook. 'The secrets of the heart are for God to know. We can only pray for the wisdom to see His love in those around us. You have been blessed with two loving parents who lived long enough to see you grown to manhood. Not many can say that in these times of war and pestilence.You're in good company, you know, being called a name like that, for showing up before you should.'

'Can't see how anyone called that is 'good company', Master William.'

'Our Lord started a good ways before Saint Joseph and Our Lady... well, they were betrothed, but before they came together, the Bible says. He even thought of leaving her over it, remember?'

'Didn't some angel talk him out of it?'

'Just so, in a dream. Your father stood by your mother whatever the truth of the situation, and he has accepted you as his true son, and his heir. One day the inn will be yours no matter what those rough louts called you. You'll be a landlord, and they'll still be barrow boys.'

'Landlord of the Angel, that's a fair enough dream for my heavy head .It's just been one long day's work into long nights at the pub for as long as I can remember. One chore after the next, and being told to smile more. It was you and your music made smiling easy ..'

They met several times over the course of that summer, in the peace of the riverside, swapping memories. They spoke of old Jake, the fiddler who taught William livelier ballads and reels. He had long gone to his eternal reward, but he'd left his fiddle to the pub. It hung behind the bar, waiting for a musician to claim it.

'My hands are too big and clumsy for that fancy fingerwork, Master William. What shall we do with the fiddle? Jake taught you, now you must do the same and hand on the skill.'

'Wait, wait, all in good time. You'll be in need of a wife I reckon, soon enough. Perhaps it's your son I'll teach if you'd spare him the time. I've taught a fair few things in my time, but never music, but to repay my debt to Jake, I'll do my best, I promise.'

Father William was as good as his word. The new young landlord married and had four children. The second son took to music. He had a good ear and once William made him comfortable with the basics, the lad soon found he could improvise and accompany his mentor or any balladeer.

So when Sir Henry's men tried to stir up witnesses around the town, regulars at the Angel and villagers from Belgrave spread the word to give the troublemakers no satisfaction. Leave the old man alone. If they wanted to help keep the country safe, there were real villains to be had up in court and testified against.

The minstrels in the market were full of songs about the

notorious highwayman John Levinson. He wasn't choosy. He robbed from anyone, drovers, butchers, shopkeepers. He dabbled in a bit of heavy-handed extortion, when he wasn't busy being a horse thief. He had already killed one constable sent to arrest him. Back in 1674 he had escaped from Wakefield gaol before charges could be brought. A few years later he was sent for transportation for his crimes and managed to jump ship. He was no easy catch, a tough customer by all accounts who had a knack for evading the law, a notorious escapee.

He had recently been arrested and placed in Leicester gaol. Leicester did not want to loose their prize so he was kept secure with multiple sets of shackles and was closely guarded.

Levinson moaned to his guards pitifully that he was dying. He requested that a few close friends be allowed to visit to say their farewells. One friend who arrived happened to be a doctor. He claimed the robber was stricken with plague, and that Levinson should be isolated to prevent spread of the infestation to the whole prison, warden and guards as well.

The thought of plague, a recurring nightmare which attacked Leicester about every ten years, was enough to panic the authorities. The shackles were removed; the prisoner was transferred to a single cell. More friends came to pay their last respects.

One happened to be an artist. He painted the tell-tale sores on Levinson. The 'doctor' declared him dead after he'd administered a sleeping draught. His friends then claimed the body for burial. Because of the fear of catching the plague, his gaolers only gave the corpse a cursory examination before releasing the it.

Levinson escaped to return to highway robbery along the Great North Road. In songs up and down the countryside it was claimed they were being committed by his *ghost*. Ghost or no ghost, that was the type of villain the law should be out catching.

Sir Henry's men had no luck. No one came forward. It seemed he was quite a favourite with the Church of England people in Leicester, and the various Dissenters and Quakers were not about to turn against 'an enemy of the state' as that was what the state thought they were too. Leicester wasn't in the mood for persecuting people for their beliefs. Sir Henry's men tried widening their search across the county; the Recusant Rolls provided known Catholic areas, and while the owners of the suspect manor houses might say nothing, their staff might want to earn a little extra. Nothing. Sir Henry would have to resort to contacting George Gilbert and hope Derby could provide something to convince a jury.

George Gilbert went through every piece of Busby's correspondence searching for any mention of William Bentney or the Byerleys. He tracked down the disgruntled Powtrell servant, Joseph Dudley and suggested he might have a clear memory of seeing the old man visit the Derby estate and, more importantly, have seen him performing christenings, marriages, baptisms or saying Mass. Gilbert asked Dudley to gather a few more witnesses, former Catholics, who could also swear they had seen Father

Bentney engaged in priestly duties. Dudley rounded up the same people who had testified against George Busby: Thomas Huis, Elizabeth Evans, Dorothy Saunders and Sarah Clark.

George Busby had had his conviction commuted and was at the time of William's arrest confined in Derby gaol. Hearing of the capture of his brother in religion, and having obtained leave from the governor of the prison, he hastened to Leicester to visit the aged captive. It seems strange that a prisoner who had been under the sentence of death should be allowed to leave his prison. It shows the great confidence the keeper had in Father Busby, no doubt aided by a liberal bribe. This monetary consideration was quite usual at this time in cases of Catholic priests and religious in prison.

When Father William was transferred to Derby for their Spring Assizes, he and Father George stayed in the same house with their counsel. The Byerleys wanted to do everything they could to support their chaplain, but for their own safety had to act through an intermediary. They requested their family solicitor, James Ludlam, also join them. James could keep the family apprised of all developments and promised to write an account of the trial to send to the Father Provincial, John Warner. Ludlam was a careful man, keenly aware of the delicate situation the Byerleys faced. James Ludlam was well respected in his profession with a tall, commanding presence and assured solemn manner. Ludlam had no illusions about the gravity of Father William's case. He saw Sir Henry Beaumont and Justice George Gilbert as the adversaries.

George Busby had tried to get his case dismissed because, having been born in Brussels, he claimed to be an alien, native of another country. A witness was brought in who swore Busby only moved to Brussels as a toddler, and Dudley spun a fine tale about Busby relating his childhood memory of being in England during the Troubles (the Civil War). Busby's witnesses who refuted this were discounted.

At William Bentney's trial, the Grand Jury 'not wishing to spill innocent blood', according to Ludlam, thought William too might have a claim to alien status. Sir Henry scotched that thought by swearing that Bentney had confessed to him that he was an Englishman. The witnesses were then duly sworn in and gave their damning testimony, virtually the same as that given against George Busby.

William was found guilty. The judge asked him what he had to say for himself. Busby had roundly defended himself in his trial, claiming the witnesses did not understand Latin and had no idea what he was doing, so could not swear he was performing priestly offices. He swore he was only saying prayers according to his duties for the Powtrell family, ie, Vespers, Matins, Evensong.

William did not try to defend himself. He replied, 'Seeing so many have sworn positively against me, I will give no other answer than that I refer myself to the mercy of the King and judge.'

James Ludlam thought the judge had been hoping for a more spirited retort, as he 'openly wished he had had more to answer for himself', brought presently the sentence of condemnation upon his own head.' The sentence was pronounced on March 13th.

Father Bentney made two addresses to the judge after the sentence was passed. Firstly, seeing that he must die, he requested sufficient time to prepare himself. Secondly, since he was 'of broken health and decayed in years', that he might not be placed in the 'common prison among the common malefactors'. The judge answered that he should have time enough to prepare himself for death, and that 'seeing he was an aged gentleman, he should be well treated, and have the privilege of a better prison.' The judge promised on his arrival in London to procure a reprieve.

This more lenient atmosphere did not please George Gilbert. This was a man whose patience was wearing thin. He had spent years trying to capture the 'treacherous prey', the Jesuits he loathed. The country need purging of their ilk. They deserved no mercy. In the interim while awaiting reprieve, Gilbert threatened the gaoler, nearly costing him his position after he heard of the leniency the gaoler had taken with Father Busby, allowing him to visit Leicester and stay with Father Bentney before the trial. The prisoners were kept 'with much rigour' and denied all visitors, but the canny Ludlam found an apothecary and the two of them were able to gain access on the pretext of administering 'physic' to them, although always in the presence of the gaoler. They were found to be very well, 'much cheerful, and well contented with their lot.'

Ludlam noted that because no evidence could be found against William in Leicester, he had to be tried in Derby. Sir Henry was not best thought of after this episode.

It may be somewhat exaggerated, but it claims that instead of the honour he had anticipated from this noble exploit, he fell into disgrace, and had to withdraw from public society, as his compeers and the gentry of his county and neighbourhood refused to associate with a man who had demeaned himself by stooping to the infamous office of informer and pursuivant. He was still in Parliament up until 1688, dying in January 1689. Perhaps those final years he spent more time at his Westminster lodgings, away from disapproving looks.

Sir Henry Beaumont's young cousin, Joseph Byerley, was the key informer. His mother Mary was concerned about his increased drinking and the late nights, or even pre-dawn mornings, of his returns from whatever tavern he frequented. He had never seemed quite right ever since the row with his father. Perhaps her suggestion of a visit to the Gracedieu Beaumonts had not been a good idea. If only her husband would encourage Joseph to take more interest in the business, give him some responsibility, perhaps then he would come round. That, she knew, was not likely since the two hardly spoke, and when they did it was to snap a jeering aside, barbs well aimed to wound.

Mistress Anne was making good progress with her classes and had become far more friendly with the staff as a result. The below-stairs gossip reached her in giggles as the kitchen scullions revealed which stable lads they fancied. It was through the girls that she learned that Joseph had come back in the wrong direction, yet rather too eager to tell the stable lad he'd come from his cousins the Beaumonts. This was no lie, as both Beaumont families were his cousins. Joseph was expecting the lad to presume he meant the Gracedieu Beaumonts and think nothing of it.

The second tidbit of servant sleuthing revealed that Joseph had received a letter sealed with the crest of the Stoughton Sir Henry Beaumont. Joseph promptly seized the letter and joked it was probably an overdue bill from his tailor. The servant who had spotted the seal drew it for Anne. She knew exactly who he'd been consorting with. As Sir Henry's men began scrouring the countryside for testimony against William, Anne went for a quiet word with Mary.

Mary thought the evidence was a good deal of conjecture and that the servants were still distrustful of Joseph, keen to see him brought down, but for all that, it did cause her to doubt her son and watch him ever more closely. She thought Charles would never believe Joseph could stoop so low, to so dishonour the family out of spite, to betray the faith he and generations of Byerleys had followed and paid the penalty for staying true. He couldn't turn his back on everything, on everyone.

Charles felt responsible for Father William. The priest his father had invited to become their chaplain,tutor, and sometime gardener was now his, more than an honoured guest, far more than a servant, almost a member of the family. He'd become a fixture that defined the character of the Byerley household. Mary had been fretting about Joseph's behaviour; mothers do. 'Young men get drunk, get hot-headed, it's their nature. It'll pass. We'll guide him to a steady wife and he can divert his energy into making us grandparents', he reassured her. Almost believing it.

Until the letter arrived from James Ludlam. Sir Henry Beaumont was questioned as to how he learned of the presence of a Jesuit priest at Belgrave Hall. 'It was the son who volunteered the information,' the MP replied, 'I believe he felt his residing there hindered their prospects.'

'Has he sought reward for this information?' queried the judge.

'No, indeed he refused any payment, saying as I was the one who ordered the arrest, I should claim it.'

Charles sat down heavily at his desk after reading this aloud to Mary. She thought he might bellow with rage but he sat slumped, staring at the words. His eyes filled up and tears rolled slowly down his lined face. Mary knelt beside him. They hugged and cried in each other's arms. There were no words.

Joseph had not returned from wherever he'd gone the previous evening. It was just as well. His parents had to decide how to face him, what was to be done with him. The family would stand by William of course, and support him, and provide whatever he needed. The judgement sentenced him to death, but the judge had promised to overturn that. Time would tell. There was no defending their son's betrayal. Now that it was public knowledge, the scandal would be a feast for melodramatic handbills. If the stories of Sir Henry Beaumont being shunned were true, their son would fare much worse if he ventured into town, pelted with rotten fruit or beaten up no doubt.

Charles thought he deserved everything that might befall him, and only wished he could think of a way to make him face up to the harm he had caused. Mary was deeply hurt, ashamed of her boy, not seeing him as a man, separate from her cradle, responsible for his actions. Mary knew their family life with Joseph was destroyed, but she wanted him kept safe, not pelted by mobs.

They devised a plan. The servants were instructed to pack his belongings immediately. Joseph would be informed that his younger brother, Charles would inherit the Hall and the business, and that Joseph had been cut out of his father's will. He could expect no less.

'I have decided,' Charles announced firmly. Mary held her breath, wondering what fate her husband had decreed for their son. 'We shall buy him a passage to the New World. He can try his luck out in the colonies and see if he can secure a future for himself where he can do us no further harm.

'Those Puritans in Massachusetts won't have him, Charles. Where can he go? Is anywhere more tolerant?'

'It's a fledgling world, but Rhode Island is said to be more accepting of all comers. Roger Williams was thrown out of the Massachusetts Bay colony and set up the Providence Plantation with tolerance his founding principle. If Joseph applies himself, he could do well. I could provide a letter of introduction and something to tide him over the first few months, then it's down to him.'

'You've had his things packed up and thrown in the barn. Where is he to go before a ship can be found? It could take months.'

'He can stay with the Ludlams in the meantime. I'm sure he'll agree. They live in the county, so he'll be out of sight, away from gossips and prying eyes. Ludlam will see to the arrangements and make clear to Joseph that our decision is final.'

Mary felt tears welling up and said nothing. She nodded to her husband and left to find some privacy in the overgrown summer house. She wanted to hold her first born, forgive him, find a way to restore their life together, turn back the past few months, pretend it never happened. She knew it was an impossible dream. She might bid him farewell whenever he eventually rolled home from this latest drunken spree, but he'd be in no mood for a hug or her tears. And that brusqueness would be the last time she'd ever see her boy, a man of twenty-two, but forever her boy.

It was some time before Mary felt able to re-appear. Joseph had not returned by noon when the midday dinner was served. This was not remarked upon; it had happened once or twice before, but it made Mary uneasy. It was a very quiet meal. The broth in porringers served with its oatcakes, the pheasant and vegetables followed by a baked tart, cheese and fruit. Charles ate heartily as usual, but Mary had no appetite. After the table had been cleared, Charles retired to the little parlour to his pipe and Mary went out to the stables. She enquired where Joseph had been spending his evenings lately, since news of the trial had reached the town.

'He heads out towards Birstall way, Mistress,' the lad told her, but couldn't say where he stopped. Mary fetched

Father Gervase, the Franciscan, who now acted as their chaplain. She feared for Joseph, she told him, since he had yet to return. Gervase Cartwright, a wise man, tried to reassure Mary that it was not unusual for young men to waste a day recovering from a heavy night. She had a mother's sense, she implored him, that this was different. 'Something is amiss. He's hurt, I know he is,' she imsisted.

To calm her he agreed to accompany her out to Birstall. They would take the cart and she grabbed linen strips for bandages, salve and blankets in case her worst fears proved true. Charles heard them setting off. He swore she was a fool to go chasing after a drunk and a traitor, that he didn't deserve her love. 'Let him mend his own sore head', he bellowed after her.

As the cart trundled on, Mary thought perhaps she was being overwrought, that she'd find her son asleep in a tavern, not pleased to be woken, cursing her, embarrassed that his mother should come to fetch him home. Perhaps they should turn back and let him find his own way, in his own time. Father Cartwright would understand.

Mary was looking for a wider stretch in the lane where they might turn the cart around when she spotted a riderless horse by the next bend. 'That's our bay mare! I'm sure that's our mare!'

Gervase gently approached the animal, speaking softly so as not to startle her. He stroked her and checked her over. It was their horse and she seemed to have a swollen fetlock. He noticed a molehill further up the lane and suspected the animal had tripped. Joseph must have been thrown.

They found him in the undergrowth. He reeked of drink. He'd fallen head first, landing awkwardly. His neck was broken, there was nothing they could do. Mary cradled her son's head in her lap and wept. There was no last sacrament for Joseph, no time to be reconciled, but for Mary's sake Father Gervase said some prayers for him. Both mother and priest silently hoped Joseph had managed a fleeting act of contrition as he was thrown. The priest tried to console her with the thought that in his state of inebriation, he would probably have felt nothing and that it would have been quick. Mary said she had feared he might have done something rash in his despair at what he had done, and at least that dreadful sin was not on his soul.

Charles said Joseph had excluded himself from a Catholic burial by his actions, but Mary insisted. For her peace of mind, he allowed Gervase to perform the funeral Mass in their chapel that evening. The Church of England, however,had to oversee the burial. The body was buried with the vicar from neighbouring St. Peter's and only the immediate family and groundsmen present.

LEICESTER GAOL

The Lord has sworn an oath he will not change.
'You are a priest for ever,
a priest like Melchizedek of old.'

(Ps. 109)

The judge was successful in getting the death sentence commuted to life imprisonment. Both priests were greatly relieved. Busby was to remain in Derby, Bentney would return to Leicester gaol. The days were warming up. The weather had brought out the pale green leaf buds on the trees as they made their way in the prison cart back to the world William knew. He was drinking in the fresh air, the broad horizon, wondering if he'd ever have this pleasure again. Fruit trees were in blossom. The fields looked well planted, with new shoots promising a rich harvest he'd not be celebrating. His bones began to ache, roughly shaken by the rutted road. A well-sprung coach would better suit a man of his age. He'd feel these bruises for days yet.

Still, he looked forward to seeing his old friends. The chief warder, Harry would be his usual gruff self, but secretly glad that old William was no slippery Levinson, plotting his escape. Harry saw little point in having to waste a cell on a decrepit preacher who wouldn't hurt a fly. He also felt uneasy having an educated man as his prisoner, and needed to prove his authority, even with his rough way of speaking, over the ancient scholar. The books Father William was allowed to keep reminded Harry of his limited education every time he checked the priest's cell. Toby, the younger guard, was altogether friendlier and more helpful. He reminded the young man of his grandfather and he saw no harm in trying to make this prisoner more comfortable. So few people of quality passed their days locked up here, that Toby feared he would soon turn as cynical and hardened as Harry, shouting and swearing at the ruffians to keep some measure of control over such a dispiriting establishment.

Leicester did not provide a vast edifice for its prisoners. There were only ever a handful of cells in a very confined area, with a central open area with a small fireplace for the guards and the warder. If there was a major disturbance, all miscreants were thrown into the tiny cells together to await justice. With such limited accommodation, Harry was annoyed to find his latest resident was ordered to have a cell apart, all to himself.

Father Gervase on his regular trips into town to minister to his flock was the first to get word of William's return. He saw that his friend was well settled in the familiar surroundings. Having been used to the company of Father Busby for so many weeks, it was good to have someone to join him in the day's prayers. Keeping his breviaries was a luxury he hadn't expected. Harry had not checked which books his new inmate was allowed.

100

Gervase was also a useful source of news. He learned of Joseph's accident and of Molly's illness. He ought to know before Becca arrived with his basket of necessities.

'At first she couldn't raise her arm for the pain it caused. Becca took over the heavy lifting while she waited for her mother to heal. It was more than an overstretched muscle. She grew worse and confessed her breast had an odd growth which she'd tried to conceal. A course of bleeding did not relieve the problem, and Molly grew weaker within weeks. She died as you went to trial. Becca is a strong woman and has had to deal with a tumultuous time of late at the Hall. I'm not sure she has had time to grieve, and it would do her good to talk to you. I know you were close, especially after her father died.' Father Gervase thought that this would also would also help William to focus his attention beyond his dismal cell.

The trial judge's instruction that Father William be well treated and kept apart from the rougher, more violent inmates only reinforced the attitude of his Leicester gaolers on his return to their long term custody. He was no threat. A kindly, educated old man who had many friends in the town made a pleasant change from their usual charges. They couldn't promise he'd be in a cell on his own, given the limited space on offer, but for as long as it was possible, he'd have his own space, and he'd be allowed his books and a small table and stool. He had thought of keeping a diary or creating a book of meditations on his confinement. The Byerleys would see that he had a ready supply of writing materials. In Derby prison, under Justice Gilbert's strict censure, he had not been allowed

101

any correspondence. Suspicions of a wild Jesuit plot were never far from from his persecutor's thoughts. Perhaps in time Leicester's rule would prove more trusting, if only to receive some measure of support now and again. To feel he wasn't entirely forgotten. His world had shrunk to four narrow damp walls and the occasional brief visits of Father Gervase and Becca.

He longed to stretch his legs in the open air, to ease the stiffness in his joints. He was used to checking on the progress of his garden; his delight in watching things grow, his joy at the beauty and the splendour of the humblest flower, had always been a kind of praying, conversing in his thoughts with their Creator. Praising, certainly, but often as not suggesting an improvement in the weather, or perhaps a less than generous appreciation of aphids and slugs.

As his stiffness increased, Toby suggested to Harry that they might risk letting William out in the yard out back to let the late summer sun soak into the old bones. There wasn't much more than a few paces to cover the length of it, but it might do him good. Becca had brought him a walking stick to lean on. Any fitter man would never have been allowed such a potential weapon, but since William was clearly frail and not in contact with any other prisoner who could swipe it off him and be a danger, the old priest was able to hobble outside, bent almost double, supported by his stick. There was no greenery within sight, but there was a precious patch of sky and the smell of the season, the tired, dried out, faded glory of August. A busy harvest-time, thirsty work, but not in town. Rubbish festered.

Flies, rats, cockroaches, mosquitoes multiplied in droves. Chamberpots tossed into badly designed street drains did not enhance the rancid air.

The borough gaol had been built in 1614 and was centrally located at the junction of High Cross Street and Causeway Lane. It was a drab building that had never been whitewashed, low-ceilinged and close. Water had always been a problem for Leicester. The river was a nuisance. The water was not fit to drink and it flooded houses every year. The Soar was neither big enough nor sufficiently below the level of the town to carry off the sewage. Some economical builders had failed to connect with the drainage system. The stench at the gaol suggested this building may have had such cut-price plumbing. It was no place for a lady like Mistress Anne to visit. A woman of Becca's station, a servant, like the cooks in the back shed, and all the men, guards and inmates, had no such choice. It was a recipe for disease.

Father William in the cobbled yard, rested on a bench and leaned back against the prison wall, letting its warmth ease his back. At the far wall a kitchen shed was a safe distance from the main building to limit any fire risk. The fuel store for their oven and the warder's hearth sat adjacent to the kitchen along the back wall. A farmer's son at heart, William had a keen eye for the weather. There was hardly a cloud in the sky, but he searched the haze above him and predicted a fair chance of a thunderstorm before sunset. It would sweeten the air, wash down the putrid gullies in the lanes, and maybe even freshen the air inside the cells, though that was a faint hope with filthy, sweaty inmates who had no kindly visitors to bring them fresh linen, who no doubt might have benefitted from the gift of washing balls of soap and a bucket of water. The air William breathed those few minutes in the yard was a blessing much appreciated. The stench indoors was harsh, a far cry from the honest country smells of the gardens and livestock round Belgrave Hall.

For all that, he was glad to be alive, glad not to have been condemned to a gruesome death. He had been spared. He had time to be a witness for his faith, to spend his days like a monk in quiet contemplation. It was a great gift. He had been lucky to have had so many years living the gentle, rather soft existence basking in the Byerleys' hospitality. He was ruefully grateful in hindsight for having been accommodated in a fine house with its own well, a blessing he had taken for granted. All the life-affirming, restorartive, rejuvenating images of water in the Bible, leapt out at him with a new intensity.

He could reassure any visitors of his appreciation of his new found vocation. Reciting the formula of being 'given the chance to retreat from the world and think only of God' went some way to convincing himself. Father William was not by nature a solitary man. He'd relished sitting in the kitchen listening to the banter, joining in. He liked being surrounded by the warmth of the baking, the smell of a roast turning on the spit, or being offered a slurp of broth, and asked for his advice on its seasoning.

Father William and Mistress Anne used to walk the paths in the garden, ostesibly choosing flowers for the house, but finding it a good excuse for discussing the latest news from London, how her literacy lessons were progressing, or the state of their friends who were ill and in need of a visit. Anne would be trying to support Charles after the double blow of his son's betrayal and sudden death. Perhaps Father Gervase will be the one Anne turns to for support herself. The old man missed her, the gentle strolls together, her lively mind and gentle teasing of his less than progressive views. It was humbling to be replaced , to watch the world you knew going on without you.

Initially he had a hunger for all the details of life at the Hall when Becca arrived. He could envisage it all, get a sense of the atmosphere, feel connected. Becca was happy to chatter away, but he could tell she was making an effort to edit her stories to keep his spirits up. New members of staff weren't mentioned, or the stresses of working for an increasingly reclusive Master Charles. She needed him to speak of her parents, Molly and Ben, to see them through his eyes. William was her link. He put aside his ache for a window into a familiar world, and comforted their daughter, editing his stories to help her.

Father Gervase had had little to do with the family, not having tutored the children or had any role in the household. He was mainly concerned with his faithful flock in the town, using the Hall as a safe place to stay, with no worries about sourcing his own food. There had been a polite distance from the Byerleys, kindliness of course, but no reason to concern him with their affairs.

As the only priest in residence, that had now changed. He had a pastoral duty to assume, to the family, the staff, those that attended the chapel and all those to whom Father William had administered the sacraments.

Over the months Gervase was slowly being measured, tested with looks and prompts, to see if he was up to the task of being their chaplain. He didn't have the refinement or education of their William, certainly, and wouldn't be able to cope with their grander visitors. He spoke bluntly and saw no shame in that. He did have a good eye for reading people, though. A priest in difficult times needed that, mixing with all sorts in the town as he was, trying to keep out of being noticed, knowing who to trust. Jesuits had a knack for looking well turned out, perhaps a little too careful about the style of their facial hair or the cut of their coat. Franciscans, although not able to openly flaunt a drab habit like their founder, still carried the tradition of not being bothered about wearing patched smocks. Wayward hair was a positive advantage in trying to blend in with ordinary street pedlars and shopkeepers. Father Gervase was not a natural fit as confidant for the Byerleys.

From the nuggets of information that Becca let slip between her jolly chats, William pieced together a rather tense time at the Hall. With gentle questioning he tried to sharpen Gervase's observations of the order of family life. 'I hardly see them,' complained Gervase, 'How can I understand or support them? They attend Mass, mumble their prayers, rattle their beads, then disappear.'

'Try and speak to Mistress Anne in the summer house after Mass. Say it's concerning your house visits. Ask after Mr. Byerley. She can speak freely there. Just listen. She's a wise woman and invaluable. What's happening to young

Charles in all this? He's the heir now. The Master should be involving him in the business. The lad's eighteen and bright enough. He was always a good student. Is his father completely ignoring him, shutting himself away like that?'

Anne wrote to William soon after this conversation. Becca brought the letter hidden in the bottom of her basket. The guards no longer searched her laundry each visit, but she was never quite sure what the rules were or whether or not they were being enforced .

Your Reverence,

I have spent my morning conversing in the summer house with our mutual friend. I am sure this was all at your behest, but it was a most welcome exchange. He has indeed a fine heart and is eager to try and fill your place, but is all too aware of his shortcomings and does not feel he will ever be equal to the task. You will always have a special place in our hearts, be assured, and our prayers rise up to Heaven daily to ease your sufferings and give you the courage to endure.

Your concern for my brother is greatly appreciated. He has withdrawn within himself and we hardly see him, as he has his meals alone. His library is his world. If I knock to ask after him, I am told brusquely that he is well. Nothing more. I am never invited in, nor does he ever enquire after me, or anyone, it seems. Mary is as excluded as the rest of us.

107

He still attends Father Gervase's Mass each morning, but stands at the back, apart from his wife and son, and leaves before anyone can greet him.

He is deeply affected by Joseph's betrayal and cannot face being seen in the town. He maintains his business by a stream of correspondence to his warehousemen. When Mary returned to the Hall with their son's body, he swore it was a relief, that the boy could do them no further harm. How can a father truly feel that? Perhaps those words haunt him now. The last time father and son spoke it was in anger. Charles still seems very angry.

Mary wrote to Gracedieu, hoping Sir Thomas might be able to offer some guidance. He and Vere stopped by in their fine carriage, on their way to visit a Dominican out at Aston Flamville.

Charles could hardly refuse to entertain Sir Thomas. The servants were sent to fetch the best Malago, that Spanish wine we only usually get to taste at Christmas, which I seem to remember you rather enjoyed. It seems to have warmed the atmosphere. Vere told Mary that she hoped the family could come for a visit to Gracedieu, that a change might prove beneficial.

Whether it was the wine or the impossibiity of refusing Sir Thomas, a visit was arranged. Charles agreed to go but as soon as the carriage left the drive, he mumbled he would find a way to avoid it. Mary let him toy with the thought of escaping, but his hand was forced. I too was included and very much enjoyed strolling round their gardens and being surrounded by the lively chatter of their splendid daughters, such a happy sound after the doleful silence at Belgrave.

Young Charles was quite popular. Mary found it a pleasant diversion to guess which young woman intrigued him most. Cicely was by far the loveliest, but the cleverest was Jane, who said little but I often caught her and Charles exchanging glances which spoke volumes. His father had no library to retreat to, so he and Sir Thomas spent hours together. Sir Thomas did not hold him in any less regard because of the actions of his wayward son. Thomas said he too felt a measure of responsibility because it was his girls who had filled Joseph's head with those wild Jesuit-demonising press reports in the journals. Sir Thomas was the one man, apart from you, of course, that my brother could confide in. I feel he will never dare to face you, for the harm his family has caused you. He makes sure you are supported and that Becca and Father Gervase have time to visit you, but I am confident you understand his pain and keep us all in your prayers, as we keep you in ours.

He could hear Anne's voice in these words. Her insight was most welcome, and refreshing in its honesty. The enforced jollity of Becca's visits or the limited interests of Gervase were not the meat and drink he craved. Ah, drink…a drop of that Malago would be heavenly. A man could sleep on the hardest pallet with a bellyful of that. William laughed at himself, 'A fine contemplative monk I am, dreaming of drinking myself into a stupor!

Filling the long hours was the main hurdle. Reading his daily Office, saying his beads, setting aside time to meditate on the saint remembered each day, praying for those who were in need of his prayers, these needed to be organised into a daily pattern to give a focus for each day. There were still large gaps. His aching body grew stiff if he stayed in one position for too long. Kneeling on the hard floor was not doing his knees any good; his well-upholstered prie-dieu at Belgrave hadn't prepared him for this. Penance, it was, 'offer it up' his mind told him, let your discomfort be transformed. Telling one's body that these throbbing joints are an opportunity for grace, does not stop them hurting, or wishing heartily for a bit of ease.

Toby was fond of the old priest, reminding him of the grandfather who'd lived with the young warder and his mother. Toby rememberd his mother helping to rub balm into the frail man's joints, how she encouraged him to keep a lively interest by chatting to him about the news swirling around the market and the gossips at the Cank Street well. She found little tasks for him, like mending a chair, to make him feel useful. She encouraged Toby to listen to his stories with respect, even though he'd heard them a thousand times.

It was obvious the old priest was finding the endless days a strain since he'd lost the companionship of George Busby. His life had always been prayerful, but it was a life based on a vocation of service to others, bringing them the sacraments, preaching the Word in his homilies, in his actions by visiting the sick, comforting the dying, consoling the grieving, forgiving repentent sinners, marrying, baptising. Active service, useful service. He could not act as a priest towards Toby, but Toby might make use of his skills as a tutor. If he were better at reading and writing, Toby might improve his lot, perhaps take over from Harry one day. The Corporation was getting more particular about reports from the prison. Harry was forever complaining about the paperwork he had to produce to justify his wage.

Would Father William agree to tutor Toby? He was delighted. There was a slight difficulty deciding which text to use as a primer. Harry had warned him not to get tricked into using any Papist rubbish and seduced into becomming one of them. Toby didn't see William as that wily, but to keep the peace, the pair agreed to begin with passages from the King James Bible. Copies were readily available and not dear. This wasn't the translation that Catholics approved of, but Father William said he reckoned he could avoid the contested passages. Toby felt it would be a great comfort to his mother if he could read the Bible to her. Writing would require a deal of practice, but Toby could sit at William's small table and try to get his fingers used to the delicate work of putting quill to paper for a portion of each lesson.

Harry thought it was all well and good to make use of their educated inmate. Harry was not a man to let opportunities slip. When Becca's basket of treats started arriving each week, he was happy to devour the lion's share, making sure there was just enough left for William to have a sample so he could thank Becca and keep the baked delights arriving. Following the trial, when it was clear that William was to be their long-term guest, it became in Harry's interest to keep William well if this supply of good things was to be kept up, so William began to receive a greater share of them. Letting Toby be tutored was just another ploy to keeping the old fellow in good humour, and his patrons pleased with Harry's care of him. Harry was sure he'd be remembered by them at Christmas.

The weather was growing decidedly cooler. William still tried to sit on his bench out in the yard when it wasn't raining, but sat wrapped with a wool blanket round his shoulders. One afternoon a cook was standing at the window of the narrow kitchen. He guessed she was peeling vegetables from what he could see, standing over a sink, he reckoned. She looked up, he gave her a friendly timid wave. She smiled and nodded. The cooks knew all about him, they had plenty of time to talk to each other about all the inmates. Harry and Toby were glad to break up the tedium of their day by regaling the women with the exaggerated exploits of the dangerous men they kept from harming the peace-loving folk of Leicester. Teasing the women was light relief. Old William was no highwayman. If he was in any way dangerous, he'd never be let out into the yard. The poor man could hardly stand upright.

'My name's Moll. You're William, ain't cha? Thought you could use a hot drink. It's only broth, mind, but it'll keep the chill off.' Moll handed him the steaming mug. He wrapped his hand around it gratefully, 'You're most kind, Moll, to think of me. I'm truly grateful. It takes me back. It seems years ago since I used to sit in the kitchen at Belgrave…loving the warmth, … delicious smells… sampling the stews, the banter.' He closed his eyes, inhaled deeply the aroma of savoury broth and seemed for a moment quite far away. Moll brushed her arm across her face. There were no more onions to chop, but her eyes were moist again.

His first Christmas in gaol was fast approaching. This was going to be a lot quieter than the twelve days of fine food and festivities he'd known in the past. Becca told him the Hall was planning a very quiet celebration this year, the bare minimum to do their duty by their tennants and business associates. After the trial, the scandal of the betrayal, and Joseph's death, no one expected the family to be in the mood for celebrating. Becca expected William would be getting a few extra visitors as Christmas drew near. The foul November sleet had made the roads almost impossible with mud sucking at boots, clogging wagon wheels, which had hindered his well-wishers, but nothing short of a blizzard would hold back his friends from seeing him over the holidays.

Becca had a quiet word with Toby, asking if he could trim William's unruly hair. It had been many months since his arrest and although the old man could manage to maintain a tidy beard, his white hair had grown to shoulder-length and was prone to looking quite wild and unkempt. Although the priest was in good health considering his altered circumstances, his unruly appearance made him seem a good deal worse. It would be a comfort to his friends if he were to appear more like his old self, and might even make him feel more at ease with his situation. William might tell all comers that he was honoured to be serving this sentence, and there is no doubt he believed this, but it was still a challenge to his mental fortitude to carry on, a strain to maintain his focus and sense of purpose.

One afternoon when the morning bustle of the lanes had died down, there was a knock at the heavy door. Harry opened the wooden cover over the small grille. A small band of rather merry carollers stood hopefully, requesting to see William. Their spokesman offered Harry a small keg of ale. A lanky lad, perhaps thirteen or fourteen, stood by his side holding a fiddle. Another brandished a tin whistle. This was highly unorthodox. Prisons do not host parties, but Harry did have a powerful thirst. A little drop of ale would ease the chill of the day, and who would be the wiser?

The revellers from the Angel were admitted and William was fetched from his cell to sit by the warder's hearth with his friends. It came as a shock to Toby to hear William's hearty laugh. The young man had never seen him smile so broadly or seem so relaxed. He was glad that Harry had decided these visitors posed no threat. The lanky lad had a present for the priest. From a sack slung across his back he brought out the old man's own fiddle, newly strung, that Becca had left with him to repair.

Neither Harry nor Toby had any idea that William had such talent. They saw him as a frail learned tutor, a gentle holy man. As he tucked his instrument under his chin and leant over, the fingers found their familiar notes. William closed his eyes and played the soulful airs his father had taught him. The lad joined in, and the piper. The low-ceilinged thick walls wrapped the harmony around them. Harry was not his usual gruff self. If he was breaking the rules about allowing so many visitors in, and his inmate out to greet them, he might as well break another and share that keg around. Toby nodded in agreement and grabbed whatever drinking vessels he could find. At a wink from William, he and the lad started on a lively reel. Feet started tapping, tables pounded, hands clapped along. It was like those Fridays back in the pub. If only the rest of the regulars could be there to swell the numbers. If only it was a Friday night at the Angel. The cooks from the kitchen shed came over when they heard all the noise, and handed round scones they'd baked for supper. 'You'll have to make do with soup tonight, William,' they teased him.

The keg ran dry all too soon. The landlord and his lad had to return to set up for their evening trade. They left William with his fiddle and a soft leather sack to keep it in. Toby promised to fix a hook up on his cell wall to hang it up safe, so long as he promised to serenade them in return. William slept well that night, worn out with all the excitement. Becca came the next day and brought a hamper of treats from the Big House, including a fine ham and a rich fruit cake. Anne had embroidered a thick, well-padded hassock as her gift, so William could kneel in some comfort. It was better than any of the well-fashioned cushions up in the garret of the Hall chapel, and much appreciated.

With his crucifix and fiddle hung in his cell, his shelf of books, writing table and stool and a feather-stuffed mattress over his slender pallet, he was more like Leicester gaol's chaplain in residence than its prisoner. He had a knack for listening, for taking an interest in everyone, for asking after them, which was the secret of his popularity. The warmth and concern he radiated was returned in simple privileges. He had a taste of fresh air, such as it was, out in the yard. Sometimes a brief respite of friendliness in the back kitchen, or on bitter days, an invitation to sit by Harry's fire. It was as good as it could be, far better than he could have hoped, but it was still a deep and painful hardship. He could not say Mass, he could not play his part in the sacramental life of the Church. Father Gervase could secretly hear his Confession and bring him Communion, which was only a risk they dared because his gaolers let them close the cell door and meet in private. If ever there were a change of gaolers, even that would be denied him. 'You are a priest forever, a priest like Melchizedek of old,' says the Scriptures, but how am I still a priest in here if I cannot function as one?

Gervase tried to persuade him that by being a wise counsellor, by modelling a prayerful life he was doing as much as he might. 'I'm not a natural contemplative, Gervase,' admitted William, 'when lads with proper vocations were racing to serve secret Masses every chance they could get, I was away tending the cows. I am a restless creature, not fit for this. I need to be active.'

The Franciscan could only suggest the denial of his

116

sacramental office was a cross he would have to offer up for the greater glory of His Saviour. He hinted that there were moves in London that might ease the plight of Catholics, put forward by the King himself.

1685

AN UNWELCOME
SUCCESSION

The Lord is close to the broken-hearted;
those whose spirit is crushed he will save.
Many are the trials of the just man
but from them all the Lord will rescue him.

(Ps.33 17-20)

Charles II had been fending off a political nightmare for
years, as the country realised he would have no legitimate
children and the next in line for succession was his
Catholic brother, James. Charles was shrewd. He sent his
very problematic brother and his wife out of the country,
removing the sight of them from provoking more hatred.
This was tactical, but appeared as a concession. He then
insisted that the Royal Succession was fundamental
to the Constitution and not a matter for decision by
Parliament. He was adamant that James, albeit a Catholic,
would succeed him, but his reign would be different. His
personal beliefs would not affect the solemn obligation
sworn in the coronation oaths to defend and protect the
established Protestant Church of England. He would also

swear to abstain from making his own appointments to high ecclesiastical office, and to transfer control of military appointments to parliament. This should reassure the populace that there was no royal agenda to return England to the Old Faith.

There were still those who felt it would be safer to bypass James altogether. They favoured passing the crown to the eldest of Charles' illegitimate sons, the Duke of Monmouth. They claim that Charles had secretly married his mistress, Lucy Walter, in Paris and that the Duke was in fact legitimate. In 1683 a group of Republicans, including Algernon Sidney, Lord William Russell and John Wildman, concocted a conspiracy to put Monmouth on the throne. This Rye House Plot was discovered and the conspirators were beheaded for treason. The government viewed this successful outcome as justification for its aggressive interference in town charters, a necessary precaution to ensure state security.

In February 1685 Charles II died. He was attended by a Catholic priest at his deathbed. James at first seemed to be accepted by the general population. When the Duke of Monmouth attempted an insurrection in the West Country, just as the Duke of Argyll did in Scotland, he was defeated, both by indifference to his cause and by his own ineptness. There was a quiet hope that time would heal the situation. James was fifty-two and without a male heir. His two daughters, Mary and Anne, were Protestant. Mary was married to the hero of Protestant resistance, Prince William of Orange, the chief opponent of France's Louis XIV and his aggressive Catholic expansionist plans.

James was no saint. He openly flaunted his mistress, yet just as openly paraded his attendance at Mass. He was not as politically shrewd as his brother though. He found Charles' rules of accommodation too restricting. He did not seek to force England back into Catholicism, but he did make it clear that he would be satisfied with nothing less than free and open public worship. The Test Act must be repealed, or he would publish a Declaration suspending it, along with other penalties for Catholics and Nonconformists.

James did not judge the climate in England wisely. Although Titus Oates had been exposed as a liar, tried and sent to prison in 1684, it did not eradicate the ferocity of anti-Cathoilc predjudice that had been aroused when his claims had first been broadcast. England would feel threatened if nuns and monks would be once again setting up institutions, if religious processions were seen on its streets, Masses openly attended. The dispensing power to make this possible had been judged illegal in 1672 when Charles had tried to put forward milder measures than James' proposals.

James wanted the same 'liberty of conscience' that Cromwell had proclaimed for all Protestants extended to Catholics. This had been withdrawn by Charles II early in his reign (The Constitutions of Clarendon). So it was that some dissenters like the Quakers were his allies. James grew less tolerant of any opposition, the universities, the bishops, the judiciary. His rants against them did not encourage a diplomatic middle way, as suggested by William Penn.

In Leicester gaol, Toby was progressing with his lessons and doing well. They had managed the Christmas stories in the New Testament, a few chapters of Genesis, Exodus, and tried to end each session with a passage from the psalms. 'There's one story in my Old Testament that's missing in yours,' teased William, 'and it's one you should know.'

'Why should I know it?'

'Because it's who you're named after, the Book of Tobit, Tobias' father. I can read it to you if you like. I promise there's no hidden Catholic message in it. It's a very old story written hundreds of years before Christ, long before there were Christians, either Catholic or Protestant. It is included in the Apocrypha in the King James Bible.' Toby nodded. He trusted William, and it was a pleasure to hear him read, to hear the words flow like music without a struggle.

Harry had been paying attention to these tutorials, hearing Toby grow in confidence, pleased with William's gentle encouragement and patience. He had a favour to ask. The Corporation had bought property across the street for a new gaol. They had ideas about what was necessary, of course, and a budget, but as a last precaution thought to consult Harry for what he might suggest. Harry was not a man skilled at writing reports. Lists, facts and figures, he could set out plainly and explain them to the Corporation, but ideas in sentences properly set out terrified him. If he spoke to William one night by the fire, could he then write it down for him? Harry knew whatever he thought wouldn't carry much weight. It was an honour to be asked.

He didn't want to make a fool of himself. 'It can't sound too grand, William, it has to sound like it's my words, but sensible like, you see.' William spent a long night chewing over Harry's ideas, throwing in one or two of his own and praising Harry for thinking of them. He spent the next two days writing up a fine report which the Corporation might find surprisingly pertinent.

In 1685, in the middle of the London power wranglings, an official notice arrived at Leicester gaol, suspending the sentence of imprisonment against William Bentney for being convicted as a Jesuit priest. A similar notice also arrived in Derby, releasing George Busby. Busby and his supporters, the Powtrell family wasted no time. In uncertain times it was imperative to make plans swiftly. As merchants they had permits to travel abroad. They had used these to help George escape when the first news of Titus Oates' claims had surfaced. George had accompanied their party as a servant. He would travel abroad again in the same manner. The training colleges abroad had been suffering since the persecutions. Their students had no support because their wealthy patrons in England were either being hounded by pursuivants or they were being bankrupted by excesive fines. Many English Catholic families had fled to the Continent and were themselves struggling to re-establish a way to survive. George Busby was fortunate in that he was a generation younger than William Bentney; he was appointed head of St. Omer's. He would survive and prosper.

William did not have such powerful connections, nor

did he have time on his side. At seventy-six he did not have a second career to look forward to. He contacted Mistress Anne as soon as he knew he was to be released. He had no wish to inflict his presence on the Byerley household, reminding them of Joseph and re-opening old wounds. He was grateful for their abiding support through these past three years, but had no idea where he might go. He felt it was wise to move away from Leicester, to a county where he was not known, to give him a chance of safety should events turn against him. Rumblings of disquiet about a king who was doing favours for Catholics did not make him feel safe. He knew the Byerleys had no permits to travel abroad, so that route was closed to him, and he knew no fishermen who'd risk smuggling him across the channel.

Anne wrote back immediately, agreeing

it would be best to be well away, and not to broadcast where you are heading. I have an acquaintance in Worcestershire, Lady Catherine Compton, who herself is a Catholic but her husband Sir William is not, so they are not on the Recusant Rolls. He attends Church services often enough to fulfill the requirements. I wrote to Lady Catherine during the trial, hoping that she might take you in if you were acquitted, knowing that with Joseph's treachery it would make it impossible for you to return to Belgrave. She was most understanding, and added that if ever we needed her home as a refuge, all we need do was contact her. I have written her this day to make preparations for your arrival.

Be on your guard. A draper's covered wagon will stop by the gaol at first light. You can rest on the rolls of cloth in the straw at the back out of sight, which is not as comfortable as a carriage, but better concealment. If anyone asks, you have out-lived your family and fallen on hard times; your great-niece has agreed to take you in. Play the old man, a little confused, a little deaf, if you are forced to speak, but it is wisest to keep silence. Lady Catherine will be able to pass messages on to me. I long to hear you have arrived safely.

Father William bundled together his few belongings, wrapped clothes around his few books and crucifix, and stuffed them into a hessian sack. He slung his fiddle in its bag over his shoulder and waited for the sound of the draper's wagon. Moll came running across the yard with a bundle of cheese-filled scones, saying she didn't know where he was off to, but it he was bound to be hungry. Indeed, if anyone pressed him, he didn't know exactly where he was going. He trusted Anne had it all arranged. The less he knew the better. Easy to play the dumb old fool if he was actually was ignorant.

It was a hasty farewell, hearty back slaps and good wishes. William hoped the report had a good response, but he wasn't eager to pay a return visit to inspect the new building. He clambered into the back of the wagon. No one seemed to be about this early. It didn't take long to find a way to carve a makeshift bed and settle down for a long trip. He placed his head behind the draper's seat so he could peer out the back and drink in the changing colours of the new day, his first day of freedom. The scones weren't long from the oven. He held them close to his chest, warm and tantalising. Just one for now. To celebrate. Heavenly. Absolutely heavenly.

The gentle rumbling of the cart, his cosy nest and full stomach soon had William fast asleep. After several hours the horse needed a rest and the draper needed a decent pie and a pint. He left his horse round the back of the inn, leading him to the water trough. William didn't dare move. The draper told him he'd fetch him some refreshment. He returned with a pasty and a half-finished pint, passed it through to William and went to relieve himself. He went back indoors and was gone for a good while. He returned with a corked jug of ale which he handed to William. The draper had redder cheeks and a relaxed gait as the warm afternoon set in and he climbed aboard. He hoped the horse knew the way, because he feared they'd both be asleep before long.

As they pulled round the front to return to the main road, a chapman called out to him. They'd obviously been drinking together and the hawker was begging a lift. It was too hot to carry all his wallets full of trifles, his sheep leather gloves and the perfumed high-topped cordevant gloves with their fine lace and gold fringe. With no longer any Puritan restraint to hinder such finery, they were selling well. Smaller pouches offered tobacco boxes, ribbons and shoe strings. It was quite an inventory as he fanned out his great coat of many pockets and kept up his cheeky patter.

The draper chuckled at his performance and mellowed by the long lunch break, patted his bench, inviting him along. William feigned sleep, hoping not to be noticed.

The chapman didn't want to go far, just to the next big town that would be worth his while. He must have glanced back in the wagon because Father William heard the draper say he didn't know his passenger. He was paid to take him along to his great-niece, that's all he knew. 'Where's she then?' the chapman enquired, 'Are you stuck with the old man for long?'

'Over Coventry way,' William heard the draper admit, 'Not too far.' If William was supposed to say nothing, hadn't Anne warned the draper too? The conversation was unusually quiet after that. Perhaps the draper had regretted his openness. Perhaps there was nothing to it. Whatever the case, the secret was out near enough.

The chapman took his leave before dusk. The draper hastened the horse to make faster progress once they were on their own. He checked to see if William was awake, 'Did you hear any of that?'

'Some,' William replied judiciously, 'Are we heading for Coventry then?'

'Not at all. I didn't trust that man after he bought me two pints and seemed so keen to be friendly. There's a lot of these hawkers earn a bit extra by spying, as they move around a fair bit and pick up scraps of information.'

'He did sound a bit too curious to me, and I admit I was worried.'

'Ah, with a little luck and a following wind I hope to get us round Coventry to a little spot called Catchem's

Corner where we can bed down at the Blue Boar before the last of the light goes. They do a decent stew and I dare say you could do with a stretch of your legs and a proper bed.'

'Sounds a good plan. Where are we headed? Will we be on the road long?

'One more night and another day after that should get us there I reckon, if the weather holds. Tomorrw we'll head over by Redditch, and try to rest at Headless Cross, which is another spot that is off the main routes. From there we'll wind our way southwest, ending up just north of Worcester. I'm to drop you at a fine place called Hindlip Hall. Do you know it?'

'No, never heard of it. I had nothing to do with these arrangements and am in your hands.' Worcester, Father William knew was in a completely different territorial district in the Jesuit organisation of the missionary province. In Leicester he had been within the college of the Immaculate Conception. In Worcester he would be in St. George's. Mistress Anne had done well; no doubt she had found a way to send word to Father Provincial.

'Well, you'll be well away from the fellows who landed you in gaol now, and let's hope we've diverted any interest in you that hawker might have had.'

'Amen to that.'

The draper was as good as his word and delivered William to the Comptons by the end of their third day. William was helped from his enclosure by two servants and rather shakily stood before a fine brick edifice that

127

boasted two towers and large windows. It was built in the Elizabethan style. Sir William Compton welcomed the priest courtesoulsy, but quickly made his apologies. He seemed awkward and was probably reluctant to be caught up in his wife's intrigues. Lady Catherine was an amply endowed lady, of Anne's generation, and Father William suspected in her mid-fifties with thick curly white hair trying to escape her tidy cap. She led him inside and directed the draper round the back to the kitchen where he would receive his supper and be shown his bed in the servants' quarters. Lady Compton had transformed a small parlour on the ground floor for William's new refuge. Anne had written to say how frail he was, so tried to arrange his accommodation avoiding too many stairs. William was quite overwhelmed with the luxury and comfort being afforded him. His eyes were moist and he kept muttering his thanks. Lady Compton must surely have thought this old man's mind was frail as well, but she never showed any unease with him.

A serving girl brought him a tray by the fire. The evening's chill after the warmth of the day made the fire welcoming and at last he felt he could relax. A fine bottle of wine with his evening supper also aided his relaxation. It was a pleasure not to be rushed. He would sleep well tonight, and must be sure to send a heartfelt message of thanks to Anne through Lady Compton for this bounty.

It was mid-morning before he woke. He had always been an early riser, but the journey had tired him more than he had expected. He listened to the sounds of the household, cherished the birdsong in the gardens that he could see from the splendid windows, drank in the freshness of the country air, and could almost taste the bread he detected baking in the kitchen. A man usually quite ascetic found himself fairly famished and after making himself presentable, timidly sought out the kitchen. Lady Compton found him there wreathed in smiles. He had polished off a tankard of ale, some cheese, a plate of smoked fish and was munching his way through a large bloomer slice.

They repaired to the small parlour after he had finished his late breakfast. William praised the house, revelling in its fine panelling.The Elizabethan woodwork had been painted in red, black and yellow to simulate inlay. Over the chimneypiece in the the Great Chamber half a dozen heraldic cartouches left no observer in any doubt about the lineage of its occupants. Down one passage off the dining chamber Father William gazed at Elizabethan arabesque scrolls painted in black on white tempura. The scrolls were twining around human, animal and bird forms. There was even a two-tailed mermaid. The family believes it is the work of immigrant Flemish artists brought up from London. Lady Compton told him the hall dated back to 1575 when it was built by John Abington, an official in Queen Elizabeth's court, to replace an earlier timber framed house. (Probably not unlike Belgrave Hall thought William, which was sorely in need of updating.) John, his wife and their three children were all Catholic Recusants. Two of his sons had been involved in the Babington Plot which was trying to replace Elizabeth with Queen Mary Stuart of Scotland.

'Were the sons hung, drawn and quartered? Some of those executions were brutal.'

'No, Edward was mercifully beheaded, and Thomas was spared due to his youth.'

'That was almost exactly one hundred years ago. I hope Thomas and his family found peace and security here in these beautiful surroundings.'

'Thomas and his wife did settle here but did not steer clear of trouble. They had the Hall adapted as a refuge with priest holes. Some of them were built by your fellow Jesuit, Nicholas Owen.'

'Owen? 'Little John'? Yes, he's quite a hero in the Society, an ingenious lay brother. A tiny fellow, not much bigger than a dwarf and blighted with a crippled leg, but what skill! He had ways of hiding priests in impenetrable recesses. He was so clever about disguising the entrances. He was also very good at keeping secret where these were. He alone was the architect and the builder. We owe him an enormous debt.'

'It was here at Hindlip that he was finally captured, you know. When the Gunpowder Plot was discovered, Father Edward Oldcorne, one of your own Brethren, was staying here. Thomas Abington and Oldcorne got word only a few days later in November 1605 that their scheme had been undone. By December, they were joined by Nicholas Owen, Henry Garnet and Ralph Ashley who were all in hiding because they were thought to be involved. In January troops came to search the hall. Abington swore there was no one here. No one was found.

'Four were hiding concealed, two priests in one hole

and the two lay brothers in another. They went on searching for twelve days. They found two empty places in the main brick wall, and three other places hidden about the various chimneys. It was in this last chimney they found two men. Apparently the chimney holes were covered with brick, mortared and fastened to planks, all coloured black to match the rest of the chimney. The hunters found eleven hiding places. The two brothers were found first. The priests held out for eight days before they surrendered.'

'Yes, they must have been starved out. Brother Nicholas was incredibly brave. They put him to the rack and still he wouldn't give up his secrets. He was tortured to death, poor man.'

'They say we may never find some of his concealments. Ingenious he was, ingenious.'

'Perhaps when you had more rest we can explore his handiwork here, if you like.'

'I'd like that very much. I never expected to feel so worn out, or so hungry. All the time I was in gaol I swore that the first thing I'd do if I ever regained my freedom, was to find a safe place to say Mass. It's what I've yearned to do all these lost years, and what do I do when my rescue comes? I break my fast and gorge myself, forgetting all my dearest wishes.'

'As the person now in charge of your well-being, dear Father William, I'm officially giving you one day's dispensation to allow you to recuperate and recover,' Lady Compton smiled as she signed the cross in the air over him, 'Tomorrow is soon enough.' He laughed, bowing his head to accept her blessing.

There was a scratching at the door. Lady Compton tutted and went to see to the would-be intruder. A fine Irish setter rushed into the room, eager to make himself friends with whomever he might find within. He nuzzled Catherine's long skirts and received a warm stroke, then the animal dashed over to William. He sat directly in front of him and placed a paw on William's knee. An invitation.

'I must apologise,' Lady Compton blurted, embarrassed, 'this is Finn. He was my father's dog. When my father came here for his last illness he insisted Finn come too. The poor dog has been lost since his death, and searches out anyone and everyone to be his new master. Finn is quite good company, friendly. Too friendly probably, not at all a guard dog. Do you like dogs, Father William?'

'I was raised on a farm, Lady Compton. My mother used to say animals liked me. Finn's a handsome animal. It'd be an honour if he adds me to his coterie of friends,' he admitted as he reached out to Finn. The dog didn't need asking twice: he leapt up, and with two paws braced on William's chest, gave him a slurpy, affectionate welcome. After a reassuring hug, Finn settled by the old man's feet panting with delight at his new acquaintance.

'If it's not too taxing, perhaps you might like a stroll around the gardens,' Lady Compton ventured , 'I'm sure Finn would appreciate a run around. At the mention of his name, the dog's ears pricked up.

'Looks like he thinks it's a fine suggestion, I agree. Reckon there'll be some rain later, let's enjoy it while we can.'

By the time they'd finished their slow tour of the planting close to the house, it was time for the main meal of the day. Sir William headed the table with only Lady Compton and the priest. He had no knowledge as yet about any other family, except Lady Compton's late father. Finn decided propping his head lazily across William's foot under the table was hint enough that any scraps would be gratefully received. The message was understood. The deal was sealed. He thought he was being discreet, but caught Sir William and Lady Compton exchanging glances after his last tidbit slipped under the table. He apologised and felt himself blushing at his age, but they only laughed and were pleased Finn had found someone to return his generous affection.

Retiring to his room afterwards, William was determined to make up for his morning tardiness by catching up with his Divine Office. He sat in a fine winged leather armchair, so much more comfortable than his cell's wooden stool. The dog curled up at his feet. He opened his prayer book and began. The delicate print soon seemed to blur. He hadn't had much drink with his food, but the richness of the food was in sharp contrast to his recent fare. His head drooped, cradled by the chair. Lady Compton peeked in, saw the old man snoring softly, prayer book on his lap with Finn looking settled at last. This was a scene she could happily describe to Anne.

This was not a new mission for William, it was a very elegant retirement home. He had the luxury of saying Mass, the privilege he had longed for, restored to him, but he was not serving a community. Catherine would attend his morning Mass, perhaps a servant or two who could be spared, but no gathering of the faithful. There was no chapel, just a plain table covered with a linen cloth in his room. Masses may well have been said here before. Little John's ingenuity had provided a panel in the side of the wooden surround of his mantlepiece. If pushed discreetly, the panel opened to reveal a narrow cupboard which could conceal a chalice and a box of communion wafers. The altar stone slipped unnoticed alongside tomes on the bookshelves. Vestments were concealed in a compartment under two wide floorboards. William felt under no threat, but out of respect for Little John's efforts, he put the cupboard and the storage compartment to their intended use.

He had to carefully assess his situation. Lady Compton had offered him a refuge; Sir William allowed her to lavish attention on an aged priest, but was not keen to be involved. He wanted no trouble. It would suit him if the old fellow spent a few months enjoying a gentle indulgence after his prison hardships, then caught a chill and died a natural death. His wife would have the satisfaction of fulfilling a corporal act of mercy and life could return to normal.

The priest had spent years in Belgrave Hall reading the mood of its masters and mistresses. He had always held a nebulous position, sometime tutor, sometime gardener, more than servant but not gentry. But he had always been a chaplain, always wanted. Here he felt it was best to stay out of the way. He prayed, read or wrote in his room until Finn nudged him to be more active. The pair would stroll the various paths fashioned in the gardens until it was time for luncheon. Often as not, the pair would retire to his room afterwards and both would rest. Lady Compton would tell him if there were any visitors expected. She never explicitly said he wasn't welcome, but he chose to take meals in his room if there were. Finn would come and go, the servants letting him out and returning him when the dog scratched at his door. One evening he overheard laughing at the dog's insistence, Lady Catherine explaining to their guests that the dog doted on her elderly uncle, who was sadly in very poor health. 'I am an awkwardness here,' sighed William.

The nature of his residence slowly began to become clear. William never left Hindlip Hall when Lady Compton or Sir William went into Worcester or rode out to call on friends. He was never paid a courtesy visit by any fellow Jesuits in the district. Anne swore they had received a message of his presence. He spent the first few months eagerly expecting to hear word of someone coming to welcome him. Nothing. It wasn't as if he was forgotten, he told himself. They knew he was safe, they knew where he was, but at his great age he was no longer any use to the mission. He was left here to die, albeit in comfort. Any Jesuit risking a visit would put them both in danger, needlessly endangering the younger man. A letter might get through. He could still hope for that much. Perhaps a message at Christmas.

William was a patient man, and a tactful one, but he had been released from custody officially. Why was there an air of his being still in hiding? Wasn't King James trying to instill a tolerance for religious differences? For Catholics being allowed to follow their faith openly?

The only person who would talk to him straight was the man he knew didn't want him under his roof, Sir William. One afternoon when Lady Compton had gone off visiting, he quietly knocked at his study door. Sir William was surprised to see him, as they usually avoided one another. His face strained to look polite and welcoming. William apologised for disturbing him, but needed some frank answers and felt Sir William was the only one who would not skirt round difficult issues. Sir William nodded, and the priest detected the faintest hint of a smile at the corner of his mouth, 'My wife is known for trying to see the most promising aspects of any situation. What is troubling you, Master William?'

'The question of my freedom,' replied the old man, 'Is it a reality or not?'

'Ah, that is a question which concerns quite a number of people at present. The King took it upon himself to release such prisoners as yourself as you know. However, there are those who protest that he had no such right, that his brother Charles had tried such high-handed manoeuvres in 1672 and it was deemed illegal. King James is making quite a few enemies with his rants. Bishops, universities and judges must agree with him or else. He may advocate tolerance, but his manner suggests otherwise. This man lacks the charm to make the allies he needs.

'Nothing is settled. Friends of the Prince of Orange are publishing pamphlets, I hear...verging on treason if what I hear is correct. I, of course, know nothing.'

'There's trouble brewing, that's what you're telling me,' gathered the cleric, 'and I must be prepared for anything.'

'Exactly so, which is why we have tried to keep your presence here more private and secluded than we might otherwise have wished. I'm sorry if my wife has not explained matters to you more fully, but she takes little interest in public affairs. She has been delighted to have a priest here and is only concerned with your comfort.'

'And I am most grateful for her care. Her consideration and her companionship has helped me readjust and recuperate with ease. I am indebted to you both. I have no wish to impose myself on this household if the political situation is as precarious as you say. I should not wish you to be placed in any jeopardy on my account.'

'You are our guest, and are free to go should you wish, but I suggest it would be hard to find another household at present as uncertain times are looming. I thank you for your concern for us, but it is probably best to lie low here as anywhere. Being on the move now would only raise suspicion, even if you could find somewhere to stay. We shall have to wait out events together, Master William, being ever more careful and vigilant, I'm afraid. I have heard there are spies and pursuivants country-wide ready to pounce on all released clergy, just waiting for the word.'

'Thank you for your honesty, Sir William. It is as I had half suspected, and I am able to prepare myself for the future having heard the facts. Please keep me informed about any developments, whatever you hear. I shall endeavor to keep myself out of the way as Lady Compton's very unwell old uncle and trouble you as little as possible. Thank you again.'

1689

HUNTED

They surrounded me, the snares of death,
with the anguish of the tomb;
they caught me, sorrow and distress.
I called on the Lord's name.
O Lord my God, deliver me! (Ps. 114)

The routine William established was pleasant and not taxing. He missed the company of being accepted as a member of the household, but Anne kept in touch with news of Belgrave. Young Charles and Jane Beaumont were married last Christmas, William's first Christmas at Hindlip. They were expecting their second child already. Time seemed to slip past the priest ever faster. Anne wrote in this most recent letter that her brother, Charles senior, had died after a short illness. She suspected he had the same weak and over-stressed heart that had also claimed his father in his fifties.

Young Charles as the new master of Belgrave Hall was full of new schemes to improve the business and redesign the hall as well. He was hoping to knock down some of the old barns at the back to create a more spacious setting for the property, and, as soon as his coffers increased, he hoped to completely rebuild the hall. According to Anne, he has been dreaming of a mansion, only slightly more modest than the Earl of Huntingdon's, the one called 'the Lord's Place, on the High Street. Anne teases him endlessly about his wild ideas. When he finds out how much his fantasy would cost, she is sure he'll have to come down to earth.

William was sad that he would not have the chance to ever see Charles senior again. He had had moments when he thought it might be possible to meet if he was free to move about openly, if he had a new posting, if, if… there would be no such freedom and certainly there would be no new postings. He could imagine the Hall decked with greenery for Christmases he'd missed, imagine the jollity, the feasting, the music, the dancing. A joyous time, convivial.

He dined in his room for Christmases here because the Compton's friends and relatives were in attendance. On several of the twelve days of the feast it was the Compton's turn to be entertained elsewhere. In their absence he took down his fiddle. There was no one to disturb. Finn sat up and seemed to like his efforts.

Thomas, the manservant who looked after him, came in quietly while the priest was hunched over his instrument, eyes shut, lost in the familiar tunes and the memories they recalled. Good times. His eyes were misty when he finished. Thomas clapped his performance, 'I didn't know you still played,sir.'

'It seems I still can, Thomas, when there is no one to object. It would not be wise to strike up a reel when I am supposed to be an uncle on death's door!'

'No, sir, I take your point. But seeing how there's none here to mind, why not step out into the hall and play for us. I could gather the servants and I'm sure they'd love it. Would you mind?'

'I'd be honoured, Thomas. Mind you, it's thirsty work, this.'

Thomas laughed, 'Every minstrel deserves his fee!' He went to fetch the rest of the staff. It was grand to see a different side to the recluse, to watch him tapping his feet and laughing at their exuberant dancing.

Thomas was another of Lady Compton's works of mercy. He had been a former slave, a house servant from a plantation in Barbados who returned to England with his master. Since he had shown promise as a lad, his owner had him educated, as a companion for his son. It was the son who persuaded his father to grant Thomas his freedom. By the time Lady Compton knew the family, Thomas was twenty-five. Lady Compton sought him out to care for her father. Employment and a fresh start, should he wish to accept. Thomas was a strong young man, able to lift the invalid should he require assistance, able to read to her father and witty enough to amuse him. Should he not care for the position, he was of course free to leave, with a favourable reference to further his future career.

When Lady Compton's father died, Thomas stayed on, looking after Sir William's needs. He didn't seem anxious to move elsewhere. Anne's request to shelter William Bentney came only six months later. Thomas was asked to prepare the same small parlour Lady Compton's father had used for a sick room for the priest.

William was not accustomed to a manservant. He'd always looked after himself. A maid could bring in a tray, or fresh linen, but a man fussing over him was uncomfortable. Thomas sensed his unease and simply saw to his requirements for his writing desk or preparations for Mass. He made sure Finn was fed and brushed free of burrs, sought out an extra rug to wrap round William's knees and left it beside his winged chair. He waited and watched.

Thomas was ready when the old man came in after their walk one frosty morning. He sat down heavily, rubbing his knees. 'If they're aching, sir, I have a warming salve that might ease them,' he suggested. William lent back and let Thomas massage the stiff joints. Another time when Thomas helped pull off the priest's boots and heavy woollen socks, he offered to bathe his feet. William found it hard to contort himself to care for them himself as he used to. Even if he could reach his toes, he would find it hard to see what needed doing. His eyesight was growing weaker. Thomas saw to everything. Walking became less painful if his feet were in good order, and his knees massaged. Thomas asked to borrow the bone-handled reading glass that Lady Compton's father had used to help William read with less effort. He knew what was needed. He had a brass tip fitted to the bottom of William's walking stick. It added just enough length to encourage him to stand taller.

As with Lady Compton 's father, Thomas was most useful in giving William someone intelligent to talk to, someone to bounce ideas off. Lady Compton popped in for Mass each morning before breakfast and they'd chat briefly but it was only pleasantries, and a list of her various social engagements. She hurried away, embarrassed that he was excluded. Even if he could detain her, Lady Compton's sunny disposition had no insight into his darker perspective and William had no wish to upset her.

Thomas, on the other hand, was a good listener and had lived through enough to have a few thoughts on the nature of freedom and captivity, of being useful and no longer needed. Thomas felt if the good priest needed him to share a glass of port after supper, it was his duty to comply and keep him company. That's how it began, humouring him. Then they started to share experiences. Respect and understanding grew, friendship. Fifty years between them. If they talked long enough, the old man would grow weary and mutter, knowing Thomas would hear, that he wished he would not see the morning. He had outstayed his welcome on earth and was a burden to all who knew him.

Initially Thomas took this as drink-induced self-pity and would help him to his bed, gently reassuring him he was not a burden, but an honoured guest. William ignored his soothing, shaking his head, carrying on less audibly until he drifted into sleep. As he began to know him better, Thomas took on what he was saying and began to argue against this misery.

'A burden, you say? Exactly so. You're a burden to the Comptons, to the cooks and maids who wait on you, and, Lord knows, you're a right royal burden to me at all hours of the day and night.' William was startled by this agreement after so many soothing denials. He sat up and gave Thomas his full attention.

'As a well schooled Jesuit, you probably overlooked the humbler tracts of St. Francis. When asked why his brothers were beggars, he replied, 'to give others the opportunities for acquiring grace.' Every single day, in every single thing you need, you are showering us with grace. For that gift I am profoundly grateful, Father William. I need all the help I can muster, so don't you go wishing our chances away like that, is that understood?'

William's eyes locked on Thomas. He reached across to grab his counsellor's hand and held it tightly. 'Understood.'

By Easter of 1688 word had reached Hindlip Hall that the Queen was obviously pregnant. After years of miscarriages, there looked to be a royal baby. The Protestant opposition were watching Queen Mary's every move. When she was delivered of a son, on the 10th of June, they declared James Francis Edward Stuart was a fraud, a changeling swapped in a bedpan to thwart the succession of Mary and her husband Prince William. It took only a week after this momentous birth for the formal invitation from the opposition to the Prince to come to England.

It took months for Prince William to muster his finest Dutch troops and find sailing conditions favourable. He landed in Torbay in Devon on the auspicious fifth of November. By the 11th of December James made his escape after he had ensured that his wife and baby son had preceded him safely off to France, the son that he hoped would be the eventual redemption of his cause.

When word reached Hindlip Hall that the King had left England, the tension in the household was palpable. Lady Compton, who never concerned herself with politics, could not stop wittering about it. 'How could a king simply leave his realm, just sail away, because his son-in-law fancies the job? It makes no sense. James has a lovely baby son, a proper English Prince, we don't need a Dutch one.' She would listen to no one, just kept repeating her astonishment over and over again.

The priest knew his position was becoming ever more precarious if James was no longer present to defend the Catholic people. Unfortunately the King's defence had been won by by antagonising everyone else. Bentney longed to return to the tolerance he'd found in Leicester.

There would be a backlash against everything King James had tried to insist upon, and the old man knew it would sweep him up in its wake. That evening Sir William knocked at his door and asked to speak with him. 'You asked me to keep you informed,' he began, 'I think you know how serious the situation is now. I think we should prepare for the inevitable. Sometime, sometime soon I fear, there will be men pounding on the door, looking for you.'

'Yes, I know. It would be easiest for all of you if I just give myself up and go out with them peaceably.'

'I have seen no reason in these three years why a good man like yourself, a man of impeccable character and of great age, should be held to be a traitor and require incarceratiion. It is a monstrous outrage and a perversion of any sort of justice. You came here for shelter, for sanctuary, and this household will do everthing possible to honour that commitment.'

The priest took a deep intake of breath, 'What do you have in mind, Sir William?'

'I propose we start training, to prepare for that impending raid. There will be very little time when we hear them pounding on the door. This is the perfect house to conceal you, but we must be swift and well coordinated. No detail must be overlooked. Are you willing to follow your brother Jesuits and lie buried in one of these holes?'

William coughed uneasily, 'I admit it is an honour I am not looking forward to. I have not a young man's stamina nor his agility. I can no longer run to hasten to my burrow either. I am willing to commence training, though, to see if it is at all feasible. If you can squeeze me into some cavity, Sir William, I cannot promise I'll hold out for eight days!'

'If the whole enterprise proves beyond you, by all means surrender openly, but I'm offering you a slender hope. We 'd like you to feel comfortable here for a goodly number of years yet, well beyond these troubles, and it would give me great satisfaction to have Little John's handiwork save another Jesuit.'

'Well, considering it's eighty odd years since he was captured here, no one who searched the house then can still be alive to share its secrets. Maybe we have a chance. Getting a plan and training is better than sitting and fretting. Let's try it. I'm game.'

After breakfast the next morning Thomas came in smiling, asking William if he felt ready to commence exploring the possibilities. It was decided that secreting the priest in any upstairs niches would take too long, given his difficulty climbing stairs. There was a cosy seat behind a wall panel in the dining hall and several compartments hidden within chimneys. The dining hall hole was accessible enough, but both Thomas and William felt it would soon be discovered as pursuivants had a habit of tapping wainscoting to detect the hollow sound of a hidden niche. It didn't look like the sophisticated work of Little John, unless of course it was a bluff, hiding a further hole beyond it. Neither Thomas nor William could detect one.

The chimneys holes were works of art. William poked his head into the tiny hatches and marvelled at their construction, completely undetectable from without. They took an agile man to manoeuvre within them, however, and the priest was fearful of soldiers lighting fires in those hearths to smoke him out. Thomas swore that Little John had built it so cleverly that couldn't happen, but William, impressed by his heroic lay brother designer as he was, preferred not to risk a slow roasting. Hiding was beginning to seem a daunting prospect.

Thomas smiled as he led William to the last hideaway on the ground floor. He knew all along that this was where the old man would most probably find a safe place, but its appeal would not be apparent until he had surveyed the other options. They started to ascend the main staircase and William demurred, 'We agreed no upper floors, Thomas. Where are we going? You know I am so slow.'

'We're here, William. No upper floors. Thomas reached down and lifted one step. A riser and tread swung up to reveal a shelf beneath the staircase. This was a common safe deposit for the family jewels in grand homes of this period. The back of the shelf revealed the entrance to a priest hole which was deep enough to sit in and long enough at its base to allow a man to lie down, although not to stretch out. There was a rush mat fitted on its floor to muffle sounds of any movement within, a close stoole(a lidded box containing a chamber pot), and a blanket. Once the priest was safely within this hide, he would conceal the entrance with the false back wall of the jewel safe.

William was helped to lower himself into position. It was not too bad. Perhaps a cushion, he suggested, 'It's a hard seat if I'm in here any length of time. How do men survive without food and water?'

Thomas nodded, 'I wondered when you'd come to that. Now that we expect a raid and have found your hole, I can keep the hide supplied with marmalade and other sweetmeats that will not perish.. You saw the small jug by the side wall?'

William nodded. There's a reed tube from Lady Compton's chamber by which you can be supplied with caudles, broths and warm drinks.

'On this staircase you are in a good position to overhear how the search is progressing, and you are concealed in a most unlikely hiding place. Wall panels and chimneys are what they'll be checking first. '

147

'And I'll be in total darkness. Where is there an any air to breath under here?'

'There's a spy hole into the Great Chamber which is concealed there by the stipled decoration and ornate wood paneling. This was one of Owen's last and most ingenious hides.'

'It'll also make listening easier, I imagine. Could you help me out now, please?' This was beginning to be a bit too real, too imminent. He felt a bit shaky at the prospect.

'We've made good progress today. Tomorrow we'll see how long it takes to get you from your room into your hole. No matter when they come, I'll be here to help you. You won't be struggling on your own.' William nodded. His bowels churned. For all Little John's cleverness, he kept thinking of those men trapped in those ungainly dark recesses for hours,days. How on earth could they stand it? Every footfall must have been terrifying. Could he really do this?

At family meals he did his best to be as bright and positive as Lady Compton. Sir William had had good reports of Thomas' progress preparing the priest for his ordeal. Sir William smiled a little but spoke only when spoken to, and then replied succinctly. His appetite had decreased markedly of late. Lady Compton 's fussing him to eat more to keep up his strength did not improve his mood. Thomas mentioned to the priest privately that he was concerned about Sir William's health. 'He has sharp pains after food, no matter what he eats. He says it's like a fire inside. He cries out at night, and I have to come.'

'What can be done? Has he seen a phyisician?'

'He doesn't want to call attention to our situation. I get him to sit up, sip water and chew a few almonds.'

'Does it help?'

'It gives him something to do, rather than just rolling, groaning and thinking the worst. If he's in pain after our midday meal, cook fixes him ginger root tea but he prefers something stronger as you know and that eats into him as well. Pray for him, this threat is taking its toll on him too.'

The priest seemed to be conversing with God more frequently with every passing day. The training Thomas directed at first had the old man speed from his bed and be helped to drop down into place with greater ease the more they attempted it. The difficult part for the old man came when Thomas lowered the stairs shut. Even in this relatively spacious box, being trapped, encased so closely in his wooden refuge, he could not stop being reminded of a coffin. His breathing became rapid. Thomas could hear him panting, 'You are fine, Father William, breathe softly. You have plenty of air and your eyes will soon adjust to the gloom. I've left several cushions in there. Can you find them? They should make you a bit more comfortable.'

He could hear the shuffling within as William dared to move and discover how he might manage so confined. 'Almonds!' the old man shouted, 'You've left me almonds to nibble on! They've never tasted so delicious!' Thomas laughed, ' You sound quite merry in there!' The trainer lent down near by William's head and spoke gently, 'You need to grow used to this place, to spend time in there so it is less daunting. I'm going to leave you here until it's midday. Knock loudly or shout out if that proves too long

149

and I'll fetch you out. I'm a hard taskmaster, not a cruel one.'

William nibbled a few more almonds, not for hunger but for comfort. He grabbed a cushion to prop his head against and decided a morning nap was the easiest way to pass the time. A rosary or two wouldn't go amiss. Later. He had hours to fill. Thomas was wise to get him accustomed to this place in the morning when there was a modicum of light filtering through the spy hole. Soon enough, he reasoned, he would need to brazen it out in total darkness throughout a long night, but he would be familiar by then with his surroundings. It was much easier being arrested in the summer house back in Belgrave Hall, than waiting in this hole. Still, it was quite an adventure. He never thought he'd be resting in the same hide that other Jesuits had shared. Traitors to some, martyrs to others. His own execution had been respited, surely that verdict still stood?

Lady Compton had been proved right. King James had not abandoned his country to its fate. He'd fled to France to raise a French army to challenge his son-in-law. In March, a month before William and Mary were to be crowned, he landed in Ireland with 20,000 troops. Tens of thousands of Catholic volunteers poured in to join his cause. James restored confiscated lands to their original owners and brought Catholics back to every branch of government. His agenda was not to grant the Irish any longed for autonomy, but to secure a foothold to the reconquest of England, and reassert his Royal Right. James' attempt to establish a Catholic court, guarded by a Catholic army meant that any vestige of clemency for convicted Jesuit traitors vanished. The priest-hunters were let loose.

The Hall had been watched for months. There was no way of stopping men having a quiet look around the exterior as they unloaded the foodstuffs and fuel that such a mansion required. Easy enough to spot an old man and his dog strolling round the grounds. Easy enough to ask a scullion or stable lad about the mistress' 'uncle'. They'd not say much, think nothing of it, but the pieces of the puzzle fit together. The pressure was on. King William wanted to tidy up the leniency of his predecessor quickly. He could not afford a network of freed Jesuit traitors making contact with the troublemakers in Ireland supporting James.

A group of five men pounded on the front door just past midnight. Others could be seen posted around the outside. Sir William and Lady Compton were not asleep; he had been suffering another gastric attack. Thomas had been attending to him. At the rough shouts at the door, they all knew the time had come. Thomas ran downstairs to secrete the priest within the staircase. Lady Compton called to the men outside that she was getting assistance to unbolt the heavy door. Thomas gave a fleeting look into the priest's room to tidy the bedcovers and grab Finn by the collar. The dog was jumpimg and barking with excitement. Thomas grabbed the animal's leather lead to control him, and securely fastened it to the frantic beast.

With Finn lunging to be free, Thomas unbolted the door, admitting the search party to the presence of Lady Compton who stood her ground with dignity. They came with a warrant for the re-arrest of the Jesuit they had reason to believe was being sheltered there. The sheriff was uncomfortable. He knew Lady Compton; she and her husband were quite influential in local affairs. He was deferential but had a duty to perform.

Calmly, Lady Compton greeted him by his first name, 'Richard, what an inconvenient time to call. Sir William is quite unwell, and is unable to greet you. He sends his apologies. Your informant is partially correct: a Jesuit had been staying here after he was released from prison, but he had sufficiently recovered to travel on…I believe he wished to visit his family in Cheshire,' she added, 'but I have no knowledge where.' The man had to respect the lady, but he didn't believe a word of it. ' So you say, Lady Compton, but I'm obliged to check, in case he's decided to pay you a return visit. I'm sure you understand.'

She nodded, 'As you wish, of course, Richard.'

The sheriff sent his men to the main rooms, prodding and tapping as expected. They poked into chimneys, checked out the width of walls, trying to sketch a basic floorplan. Men were sent to the upper floors, to the attic space. All the servants were hastily assembled in the main hall, terrified. One look from Lady Compton, as she was escorted to be with her husband, told them they had better say nothing.

The troop spent several hours stomping through the house, shouting to each other whenever they thought they'd found a priest hole. They managed to find several, but they all were full of cobwebs, not an aged Jesuit. Eventually the sheriff gathered his search party, informing Thomas that he would be posting a guard to surround the house overnight and return with the rest in the morning to conduct a more thorough investigation. He asked Thomas to convey his regret that they disturbed Sir William when he was unwell, but he was only doing his duty, and hoped the matter could be resolved swiftly.

The priest, concealed within the main staircase, could hear every word. He reckoned they'd return quite early. There'd be no point getting pulled out, especially as his guards will be listening closely to all household noises. Thomas hastened the staff away to their beds to gather what sleep might be possible. 'Go straight up these stairs,' he instructed them, 'Don't waste time going round the back stairs tonight.' Old William cringed as he felt their footsteps shudder the treads inches above his head.

After they were well out of the way, Thomas bent down to whisper to William, and check how he was bearing up. The priest only had one request, 'Can you leave a candle in the Great Chamber? A sliver of light would mean a lot, but only if you think it wise.'

'I think that would not cause any undue suspicion. Try and get some sleep.'

'Bless you, Thomas. I'll try not to snore!' It was an attempt to sound braver than he was. His legs desperately wanted the freedom to stretch out and change position. His calf muscles tightened with cramp. He wasn't sure the chamber pot would be able to cope with the urgency, the frequency. Those other Jesuits were young men in their prime. Just thinking about the problem made it worse. 'God help me! I'm not cut out for these heroics, Dear God, please let it end soon.' He doubted whether he'd get a wink of sleep.

As it happened, he dozed off fitfully, waking when one buttock or arm or leg turned numb, shifted a bit, drifted off, then re-awoke to pins and needles. He was weary and sore. He had more than made up his mind to give up when the search party returned. Sir William was up and dressed, ready to greet his intruders, as gracious and calm as his wife had been the previous night. He offered to provide refreshment for their thirsty work. The sheriff was appreciative, but declined his hospitality.

The man had no wish to linger. He strode determinedly into the small back parlour and spent a good deal of time assessing the scene. From the prayer books on the shelves, the crucifx on a prominent table, a sick bed, he deduced this to be the priest's room . Thomas had removed the chamber pot so there was little evidence of a recent occupant. William's bed would be cold. There had been no time to change the linen, however. Richard smelled tangy sweat on the pillow slip, and found long grey hairs. He paid special attention to the chimney and while no priest hole was discovered, he did open the side panels and found the chalice and communion wafers. Lady Compton tried to explain them away, saying they were kept for the use of any visiting priest. She was known to be a Catholic, finding these should come as no surprise.

'No, indeed, Lady Compton, but finding dirty linen when you claim the priest left years ago, that does surprise me.'

He knew the man was on the premises, probably such an old man couldn't have gone far. He noted Finn's basket by the hearth. 'Bring the dog here,' he ordered.

Thomas feared this approach, 'The dog is not well trained. He's capricious, unpredictable, sir. I would be concerned he might attack you as a stranger.'

'Bring it here.'

Finn was delighted to escape the confines of the kitchen. Richard smiled when he saw how harmless and friendly Finn was, stroking and speaking gently to him, 'Now then, Finn, your master's gone missing. You're the only one who can find him. Let's see if you can do that for me, heh, Finn.'

Richard led the dog around the room. Finn took no particular interest in any spot, excepting his own basket. Having checked there was no trap door under it, Richard guided Finn out into the hall. 'Let's see where your nose will take you, old boy.'

Finn bounded about, free of the leash. He sniffed at the sheriff's boots and the muddy tracks left by his men. The dog traced their route to the stairs, and started to follow them to the first floor. He stopped near the top and began scratching and barking wildly. Thomas knew the game was up.

Both he and Richard approached the spot. The sheriff motioned to Thomas to open the secret hideaway. Two steps were swivelled upwards to reveal the priest with tears streaming down his face. Finn leapt up to lick them away, delighted to see him. William buried his head in the auburn curls, hugging the animal, praising him. 'You saved me, you wonderful fellow, I couldn't stand another minute in there, good dog.'

'William Bentney, I'm afraid you must come with

me now. King James did not have the power to suspend your sentence. You're to be returned to Leicester gaol in accordance with your original conviction.'

Lady Catherine and Sir William were summoned. Thomas helped the priest out of his hole. He was too weak to stand unaided and in need of a good wash and fresh clothes. Sir William touched Richard's arm for a quiet word. 'Now that you have your man, there's no hurry. You can see how frail he is. This priest is nearly eighty. He will never survive the journey back to Leicester if you don't let him recover first. Let him have a good meal and a proper night's rest after he's cleaned up. You can keep an eye on him easily enough, we'll do whatever you require, but just look at that wreck of a man and have pity.'

Richard considered this for a moment or two, watching Thomas nearly carrying the cleric back to his room. 'Clean him up, feed him up,' Richard conceded, 'I know he's no common malefactor. He deserves some dignity, but I can't delay overnight. We'll pack him off in the cart after he's eaten, but I promise to try and make the journey as reasonable as I can. That's all I can do.'

A couple of hours' grace was all it amounted to. Lady Compton promised to pack up his belongings and get them sent on to Anne. She would be able to negotiate with the gaol to see what his new gaolers would allow. If he were restored to Harry and Toby's care, there would be no problem, but there was a new gaol now and a new king. Nothing was guaranteed. William didn't know what awaited him.

1690

LEICESTER

I will hear what the Lord has to say,
a voice that speaks of peace,
peace for his people and his friends
and those who turn to him in their hearts
                                        (Ps. 84:9)

The new regime seemed to be redefining its role, to secure its position and allay Parliament's fears. It reiterated the Crown's commitment to reforms to limit its powers: No more standing armies, no dispensing power(which had freed the priests), no resort to extra-parliamentary taxation, no special courts, freedom to petition guaranteed, free elections and annual parliaments. In that same spring an Act of Toleration was passed.

Its title sounds more promising than it actually proved to be. Freedom of worship was granted to those Nonconformists who had pledged to the oaths of Allegiance and Supremacy, and rejected transubstantiation, ie, Protestants who dissented from the Church of England such as Baptists and Congregationalists, but not to Catholics. It purposely did not apply to Catholics, nontrinitarians, or atheists. The Act also continued existing social and political disabilities for everyone who refused to attend and take Communion in the Established Church, including exclusion from political office and from attending universities. The new King was using this Act to consolidate his support with Nonconfomists, to show he was a better ally than James.

It took several days to arrive in Leicester. Along the route the sheriff secured comfortable accommodation for William in various inns and realising the old priest's infirmity, decided to dispense with manacles or any other physical restraint. William was grateful to be spared that indignity. They dined together, conversing easily, and an observer would not suspect this was an officer of the law with his prisoner. Richard asked how the warders in Leicester treated him, worried that this frail man would not cope with a harsh regime.

'It was not unpleasant,' William reflected, 'and they did their best to ease the restrictions that any confinement entails. The judge at my trial said I was to be treated well and kept apart from the rougher types. When I first arrived, this ruling was scoffed at, seen as a nuisance. The old site was cramped enough without me requiring to be kept separately, but once they realised I was clearly no troublemaker, and in no fit state to make my escape, in time I was trusted, and I might even say, befriended. If my gaolers, Harry and Toby, are still in charge at the new premises, I will have nothing to fear. They are good men. It'll be a curious homecoming.'

Richard seemed reassured. He'd never heard a prisoner speak so reasonably of his warders, but then again, he'd never escorted a prisoner quite like William. Something was troubling his dinner companion, though, if it wasn't the gaol or its staff, what then?

'What have you heard of this new king?' William asked very quietly, 'I understand the strategic and political point in overturning King James' leniency in letting us go, but will he take it further, do you think?'

'Further? How?'

'Will he overturn my commuted sentence? My death sentence was respited by the court, not the king. Does that still stand?'

'I'm just a lowly sheriff, not privy to the new king's plans by any means, but as a monarch invited over to replace a high-handed one, King William, it seems to me, is trying hard to show his respect for Parliament, to garner all the support he can get, especially with old King James snapping at his heels in Ireland. Rounding up papists and locking them up keeps you lot out of mischief. He doesn't need the extra nuisance of challenging the courts. Leastwise, I think he'd be a fool to try.'

'I hope so. Can't see the point myself, but in uncertain times, when you've heard a death sentence read out to you once, you can't help thinking it could happen again.'

'I can't see that executing a gentle man like yourself, a man of great age, would do anything but turn public opinion against him, which is the last thing he needs. Rest easy, William, Leicester will look after you and keep you safe from harm.'

As soon as the sheriff departed, Lady Compton was busy. She had Thomas pack up all William's belongings, adding a few more books for good measure. She instructed the cook to pack a generous hamper of treats, enough to indulge his guards and make sure some would actually reach the priest. She selected the warmest blankets, sturdy cushions and a boxful of writing materials. Lady Compton sent off a hastily written note to Anne to tell of William's recapture, and not waiting for an invitation, announced she would be arriving at Belgrave within the week to make certain Father William was being 'properly attended to'. Lady Compton had heard little from Anne over the past few months and hoped her friend would not be too inconvenienced by her sudden arrival.

Anne made few demands on the social world of Belgrave. 'Young' Charles and his wife had their own friends and she did not feel it right to impose herself on her nephew's world. They worried about her and would no doubt be delighted that Lady Compton was paying her a visit. The present master of Belgrave had been eighteen when William was first arrested and dragged away from the Hall. Now Charles was married, a father, running the estate and the business. He had little time to reflect on his old tutor and chaplain.

Until recently, Father Gervase had seemed to manage well enough. Only he, too, had fallen under suspicion lately and had been taken in for questioning. When the children were older, perhaps another Jesuit might be requested to teach them, but it was not a thought uppermost in Master Charles' mind. He assumed Anne had taken over responsibility for maintaining the imprisoned man after his father died.

Her securing a place for William with the Comptons had been a great stroke of luck. It had seemed far enough away so that he would not be recognised by any Leicestershire searchers, but in turbulent times, any lone male visitor to a known Catholic household was bound to arouse suspicion. Perhaps that chapman who shared his outbound cart had tipped off the spies years ago, and the information was stored away, waiting for the right moment. The spies had waited years to pounce on George Busby in Derby in that first wave of arrests; if they'd known ever since his release where William Bentney had fled, they only had to bide their time. Still, for three years the old priest had had a soft bed, good food and pleasant surroundings. He had had no congregation as such beyond the household, but he had been able to say Mass daily, the freedom he cherished most.

When Lady Compton arrived at Belgrave Hall she was greated warmly by the whole family, and Becca laid on a splendid repast to honour the lady. Afterwards the two old friends retired to Anne's private withdrawing room. Lady Compton noticed Anne's health was a serious concern. Her left arm rested listlessly on her lap; she had received discreet help from the serving staff during the meal. Her speech seemed to require more effort. Even if her writing hand was not impaired, clearly the woman had been afflicted and was having to adjust to a greatly changed way of life. No wonder she had not been corresponding regularly.

Anne acknowledged Lady Compton's concern by

admitting she had been unwell, quite frightened in fact by the weakness that overtook her, but assured her friend that slowly she was regaining some of what was lost in the initial attack. Unfortunately, the effort to recover was proving very taxing, and her need for sleep seemed more like that of a newborn these days.Lady Compton took the hint, suggesting that the long journey had tired her and rest would be a most welcome restorative. She looked forward to a turn round the gardens with Anne in the morning, if Anne felt strong enough.

On settling in to her own room for the night, Lady Compton reflected on her friend's condition. Anne did not strike her as a woman recovering, rather as a woman fading. Her eyes were dull, her every thought a great effort. She doubted whether the woman could withstand another such attack. This was not someone who could be entrusted with the responsibility of maintaining a prisoner, of foreseeing his needs, and placating his gaolers. Simply getting through one day at a time was as much as her friend could manage. This was going to be a very short visit she decided.

Early the next day, she had a word with Charles in his study. Charles was quick to see the difficulty. He, too, thought his aunt was too delicate to cope with any duties save her own welfare at present. Charles assured Lady Compton that Father William's upkeep was his ultimate responsibility, but in any practical sense it was down to Becca who had managed it so well in the past. He called for her to attend them, and properly make Lady Compton's acquaintance. In front of both women, Charles reiterated

162

his promise of continued support for Father Bentney, and his gratitude to Sir William and Lady Compton for their years of care for his old tutor after King James had released him, 'Anne frequently reported how well he was and how kind you all were. She mentioned Thomas and Finn especially, I believe, as well as your good self, of course.'

Lady Compton laughed, 'Thomas was his manservant, and Finn was his dog, an Irish setter that never left his side. I'm sure he'll be missing them both.' Lady Compton mentioned that she had travelled to Leicester with a number of William's belongings and was wondering if Becca would know if the gaol would allow him to keep them in his cell. Becca smiled, remembering how leniently William had been treated before. Charles had no idea. He suggested Becca accompany Lady Compton to the gaol as she knows the warders.

Becca thought the sight of the Compton's fine carriage with its coat of arms on the side and liveried footmen pulling up outside the prison was persuasive enough and doubted her humble face at the grille in the door would carry much weight. She would never get a chance to ride in a carriage like that again, so very different from Tom's cart. She happily agreed. Lady Compton nodded, equally pleased. Speaking to Charles had been a necessary formality, but the real person who'd be looking after William was Becca. This was the woman who would make her long journey worthwhile.

In the privacy of the carriage, Lady Compton could talk more frankly about Anne's condition and her fear that Father William would be forgotten. Becca explained how she had known the priest since she was a child, how he'd taught her to read and was a great comfort to her and her mother when her father died. He'd always looked out for her, and it was time she looked after him. She giggled when asked about the gaolers. It wasn't something she could say in front of the master, she didn't want anyone to get into trouble. Father William would have had a much harsher time of it if word had got out, but he had been treated treated more like a lodger than a prisoner, kept away from the rough types, and even allowed to sit by the warder's hearth on winter nights, or out in the yard for a bit of fresh air when the weather was fair. They had let him grow a few tubs of plants out in the back corner. Before his release he had been teaching Toby how to read and write, and was scribing for the warder, helping him keep up with the reports the corporation required.

Lady Compton nodded, not at all surprised how well William adapted to prison life, and how well he was accepted. 'He's a man who's easy to like,' she smiled.

'And easy to love,' added Becca softly.

They pulled up outside the imposing building, Three storeys tall, five windows across. Each window had a stout iron lattice so there was no doubt about its purpose. The carriage did impress the guard who answered the door. Toby almost didn't recognise Becca when she emerged from such grandeur. She quickly explained. Toby called Harry over. Since it was a quiet day, no court officials coming and going, they quickly hauled in the goods Lady

Compton had brought. William was kept strictly confined when any outsiders entered, and was seen to have no particular privileges, so long as no one looked too closely into his cell. Lady Compton stepped inside briefly to speak with Harry. 'I wish to be informed if there is, for whatver reason, any change in the circumstances of his support from Belgrave Hall. I will happily take up that responsibility should the need arise, do you understand? And of course I shall see that you are handsomely rewarded for keeping me informed of any changes in that respect. Can I rely on you?' Harry was as meek as a lamb in her presence, nodding agreement repeatedly. A far cry from the surly foul-mouthed bully who barked at his less pleasant charges. The lady swished her silken skirts swiftly out the door and was helped into her carriage. Becca asked to remain a bit longer and said she'd walk back to the Hall.

William had only greeted Lady Compton from his cell. The door had been shut as it was whenever someone called. She spoke to him through the small grille in the door to check he was well. She was uncomfortable in such surroundings, and eager to be away as quickly as possible. Lady Compton was a determined woman, determined to do her good deed, but friendship was not something she associated with priests. Respect, honour, reverence. That was what was called for.

When she left, the cell door flew open. Becca rushed into William and gave him a resounding hug. She was crying with delight at seeing him, mixed with the bittersweet knowledge that it was possible only because he was re-arrested. The old man had been given manly, reassuring pats of welcome on the back from Harry and Toby, but he had not held a crying woman in his arms since he'd consoled her mother, Molly, after Ben had died. Was that near on forty years ago?

He stood back to look at Becca. She was a woman in her prime still but the grey hairs and lines around her eyes spoke of decades of hard work, long hours in Belgrave Hall's kitchen. He'd watched her grow up, cooking alongside her mother, caught her smiles when he basked in the comaraderie of that kitchen, loved the sound of her laughing. Was there any laughter left with her mother gone and a cohort of scullions to supervise?

Becca tried to question William about his immediate needs, but William was more interested in finding out how life was treating her. Outward looking, thinking of others, listening, that's why people took to him. Becca's cheeks flushed and a broad smile transformed her. 'I'm getting married,' she blurted out, 'I couldn't wait to tell you!'

'Married, heh? That's wonderful, Becca. Now that poor chap just wouldn't happen to be the same man you've been teasing for as long as I can remember, big old Samson's eldest, John?'

'Of course it's John, who else would I give the time of day to? John took over the blacksmith's just about the same time you were being tried. Of course I've known him forever, and when his younger brother Tom came to help you in the garden…well, you know how we used Tom, but I couldn't risk losing my position at the Hall.'

'So what's changed?'

'I've changed and life at the Hall has changed. I would like the chance to have a full life, a husband and home of our own, not lonely in an attic space in a grand house. The master is dissatisfied with the place. He wants a 'proper brick mansion' with expansive gardens, not the cramped ricketty old Hall that's always in need of repair. I reckon they're planning to sell up and move because there just isn't the room in the village for the grand place he dreams of. I can't see myself moving with them. My life and the people I love are here.'

'Will you stop working at the Hall after your marriage?'

'I'm training Kate to be my replacement but hope to step down and assist her as and when I'm needed. We work well together, but I'll have to bite my tongue to let her give me orders! Leastwise I'll still have some income to ease me into my new life.'

'What do the Byerleys think of your plan?'

'Master Charles is happy for me, he says. Frankly, since I've saved them the trouble of hiring a new cook, I don't think he cares. Mistress Jane is more understanding. She even hopes John and I will start a family. She thinks it's not too late to hope, but I think that's a dream too far., but it was kind of her to wish it.'

'So when are these nuptials planned? It seems like you two have waited long enough.'

Becca giggled, 'Long enough, nearly a lifetime it feels. We would have liked a priest to tie the knot, but that's not allowed. We want it to be official so we'll be married by the vicar in St. Peter's. It's set for the end of June, the feast of Saints Peter and Paul.'

'Well, I'm sure either Father Gervase or I would be delighted to give you both a blessing if you could pay me a visit.'

'Hasn't anyone told you? Father Gervase is in here too! They rounded him up just weeks before they found you. They don't usually bother with poor Franciscans. Maybe they thought he was a Jesuit too. Anyway, you'll have a friend here when you're strong enough to get up and about.'

'It's been rather hectic settling in here, and with so many outsiders coming and going I've kept tucked up in my cell, and Toby and Harry haven't had any time to stop and chat. Toby dug out my old desk from a store room, you see? And I understand you are the one I've to thank for a new stuffed mattress. It's very welcome for old bones I assure you.'

'Toby got word to me as soon as he knew you were on your way. The kitchen girls and I whipped it up one night. Such a slim pallet doesn't take much sewing or much stuffing and a pitcher of ale made it a jolly evening. The new girls wanted to hear all about you.'

'Glad I could be the excuse for a pleasant night's work! You've gone to so much trouble looking after me over the years. Now that you'll have a husband to look after I hate the thought of you wasting hours dragging yourself into town to see to me, wearing yourself out...'

'Don't you fret, William, it's my pleasure. Doubly so. Either Tom gives me a lift in the cart, or John comes over if he's not busy and we'll walk in together, most likely having to stop for a pint before heading back too. The thought of those afternoons doesn't wear me out at all, quite the opposite,' she blushed.

'I see, I shan't worry then, but listen, dear Becca if ever you do need a rest or you two can think of better things to do than walk into town, just send Tom along with the basket, you promise?'

'I promise.' She gave him a squeeze of his hand as she bade farewell. Another hug would be too much. She could sense it had startled him, pleased him, but was not to be repeated.

Toby came to his door with a tray, 'Moll says we're to feed you up, that those rich folks will have spoiled you and given you a great old appetite and she'd not have your friends think we're starving you here.' He set down a steaming bowl of chicken broth and several hot buttered cheese scones.

'This smells grand, Toby. Please thank Moll for me. She remembered I love her cheese scones! She gave me some for my wagon trip out to Worcestershire, still warm they were. I cradled them close, savouring the smell. She must have been up before dawn to get them ready in time. I had no idea where I was being sent or who might want to find me again, but Moll brought me her scones to wish me well. It meant a lot that kindness. Please thank her.'

'You can thank her yourself tomorrow. I'll give you the grand tour after breakfast, but once you've finished your broth, I reckon Gervase would like to drop by. Evening prayers is what he was going on about.'

Gervase knocked at the partially open door. William was delighted to see him, but worried as to why he too had been arrested. 'I reckon the sheriff was under pressure to be seen to be doing something, and rounding me up was second best to finding you.'

'See that's what comes of tidying yourself up to live in the Big House: they take you for a high-living Jesuit!'

'Maybe so, maybe so. I have grown scruffy in here, so perhaps they'll let me go. The Byerleys are doing what they can. Mistress Jane's family, the Beaumonts, have more influence. We shall see. Meanwhile, we can keep each other company. You seem to have been a bit of a favourite here in your time. You converted them all: not to Catholicism, but to at least admitting Jesuits are not the devil incarnate! That's progress! Your reputation has made my stay much pleasanter I can tell you! I wasn't sure what to expect.'

'Were you given any rough treatment?'

'No, not really, my own fears were worse than anything that occurred. I was questioned rather strenuously, and at all hours. They were determined to find you and were convinced that I was in contact with you, or some of the family were, since they'd been supporting you. I said I only knew you were out of the area and hadn't had any contact. I knew the family had stopped any contact after Mistress Anne became ill. Master Charles had delegated all responsibility to his aunt, and she was beyond questioning in her present condition. They daren't risk putting her under pressure, so I was their scapegoat I presume.'

'What charges have they brought against you?'

'Nothing yet. So far as I know no one has sworn against me, and since you've been found, I'm no longer of much interest to them, or at least I hope I'm not, if you don't mind me saying so.'

''Not at all, dear Gervase, I'm used to being their fox. The sooner they let you go, the sooner you can help poor Becca and John prepare for their wedding. Lord knows, they've waited long enough!'

Toby collected William the next morning to show him round, as promised. It was a slow business as William needed to stop and catch his breath. The new brick edifice smelled fresher than the old gaol. It was built with care, with the warder's hearth, office, a surgery and stores rooms on the ground floor. A few cells were kept apart on this level, for the better class of prisoner or for any women. Strong barred gates blocked access to corridors lined with cells. There were stronger doors, better locks and plaster floors. Cells differed in size, but most were eleven foot square. Staircases were positioned in the centre of the forty foot long edifice. It seemed a good deal more substantial and forebidding. The ceiling height became meaner in the upper floors; ground level luxuriated with eight feet, the middle only seven, and the poor souls on the top only six. Galleries in the loft afforded more storage space.

When it came to the upper floors, William looked worried. Toby had anticipated the problem. He called over Jimmy Norrice, another gaoler. Jimmy was broad as a barn door, a beefy fellow who was usually dressed in a loose hip length leather jerkin, which emphacized his sturdy frame. 'The old priest needs some help getting upstairs, Jimmy,' Toby explained. They'd obviously already come up with a plan. Jimmy assured William he would come to no harm, then bent down and slipped the old man across his shoulders, grabbing his legs with one arm and pulling William's nearest dangling arm with his own free arm to secure the priest's position. He told his passenger he was as light as a kitten, and brought him safely to the next landing in a trice. William felt giddy as a child, delighted by the surprise lift. Jimmy and Toby thought their scheme had worked quite well and congratulated themselves.

Upstairs another hearth for a guard's post and a long corridor for the common riff-raff. At the back of the building was a small yard, similar to the design of the previous gaol, for taking delivery of goods, refuse collection, and allowing access to the new kitchen, now housed in a decent brick outbuilding. William noticed the door to the kitchen was framed by two of the potted roses he had nurtured. Someone had pruned them well. They were doing splendidly and were a feast for the eyes after the harshness within. The cooks insisted on their bench just by that door, to grab a few minutes of cool air when the ovens were fired up. Moll was just coming out, hoping to enjoy her pipe in peace. William waved to her, and she came lumbering over to greet the stooped priest resting on his walking stick.

'Look at you then, Father William, come all this way to feast on my cheese scones! Didn't they feed you up out there with them fine folks?'

'Oh, they fed me well enough, Moll, but their cooks lacked your magic. I'm under your spell, Moll. I'll stay here forever to be charmed by your cheese scones!'

172

'Get away with you! You'd soon get put out living on just my scones. Wait till you try my fish pie this noon. That's a proper feast on yer plate, that is.'

'I can only hope the morning flies by so I can relish it all the sooner!' Moll laughed at his elaborate flattery, the old game between them. In a life spent taking gruff orders from employers, and barking equally harsh commands to her scullions, hearing fine words of praise, even in jest, changed the music of her day. William nodded his farewell and asked Toby to guide him back to his cell for a rest.

As both clerics suspected, Gervase was not detained much longer after William was re-arrested. There were no charges. He returned to Belgrave Hall as their chaplain, and no more questions were asked about whether or not the Byerleys were involved in William's escape to Worcestershire, or had kept in touch. Becca reported that Anne had had another attack and could no longer speak. Her left side, both arm and leg were now affected, so she was confined to her room and required constant attention. Charles has engaged a woman from the village to look after her. The physician told him to expect another attack soon. She is not likely to see Christmas, he reckons.

Becca and John were wed by the vicar in a brief ceremony on the feast of Saints Peter and Paul at the end of June. There followed a Mass in the garret chapel which had been adorned with abundant flowers from the garden. Mistress Jane had presented Becca with a dress length of lovely dimity that Becca had been allowed to choose. Jane's own seamstress made it up for her. Master Charles sent

173

John money for a decent coat, breeches and a new shirt, so Becca would have a smartly turned out groom to match her finery. Mistress Jane's maid helped Becca arrange her hair, with several rosebuds pinned neatly to frame her starched cap. After Father Gervase's Mass, the happy pair were driven to the gaol in the cart now bedecked with ribbons.

William had never seen Becca look so lovely. Harry ushered them into his office to receive the priest's blessing, far better than crowding his tiny cell. The blessing only took a moment, then the gaolers produced a flagon of ale to toast the newlyweds, and Moll brought a tray laden with 'Valentine Buns' which William had told her Becca's mother had been famous for. It was only light refreshment to break their fast for they had a feast to return to at the Hall, but it was much appreciated, transforming a grim prison visit into part of the festivities of a joyous day. As the couple departed, William accepted a brief hug and kiss from the bride as he whispered in her ear, 'Don't you come back here for a fortnight, do you hear? Enjoy yourselves, God bless you both!'

With Gervase back at the Hall, William had no companion. He kept up his daily prayers, but otherwise read less and slept more. Toby often would look in on him and find an open book propped on his chest and the old man snoring softly. He had to be encouraged to walk about to ease the stiffness in his limbs. Harry at his desk would hear the clink of the heavy barred door to his corridor after breakfast and know that was Toby fetching the old man. Soon his shuffling feet could be heard and the tap of his walking stick, heading for the bench in the yard, or at least a stroll around the ground floor.

Few men had lived as long as William. Harry and Toby took pride in the fact that their care had kept a frail man so lively for so long. Moll was convinced it was down to her cooking. William thought they all should take credit, but should share it with the three monarchs who decided to cut down on his workload and insist on his abrupt retirement. William was a man who had always wanted to be useful, to serve others. He would have preferred to do this through his preaching, adminstering the sacraments and charitable works of mercy, but for years his priestly vocation had been curtailed. Toby understood this good man's talents had been wasted. This man should not doze away his final years, dulling his mind.

A prison at night is not a quiet place. Even in a solid brick building, the cries of the desperate, wretched inmates can be heard by all. Those whose sleep is disturbed swear and shout down the miserable. Some are plagued by nightmares, fear of what they've seen, or done, fear of the hangman's noose, or the whipping post.

Old men sleep fitfully. The early hours before dawn the body decides is time to be wide awake. Two in the afternoon is a far better time for repose, after a full meal. Big Jimmy Norrice usually worked nights. He was capable of dealing with any rowdy drunkards who might need a night in the cells to sober up.

Jim had often seen William lying awake, even before the screams and shouts from upstairs had begun. He mentioned it to Toby, who put a suggestion to the priest that if he was willing, he might comfort those men and ease the terrors of the night. He might bring peace to some very tortured souls, if he felt he could.

William was immediately interested, but naturally wary. There were burly murderers awaiting trial up there, not shaken penitents. Some were clearly madmen. Toby assured him that a guard would be right outside the cell door whenever he was locked inside with one of the troubled convicts. He was free to refuse to deal with any prisoner he judged a danger. He was free to refuse to even consider the idea at all.

He prayed about it, laid his fears before the Lord, and decided to see if he was any use, if the grace to say the right thing would be granted him. Jim would see he was transported upstairs effortlessly. He sat with a young man who had killed his father. The lad had been trying to defend his mother and the rest of the children from his father's drunken rage, but the jury still decided he should hang. As the story unfolded, the lad hadn't stopped a vicious attack, but had smashed the man's head in after he'd passed out. The youth was terrified and filled with remorse, but convinced he would do it again if faced with the same situation. Father William listened to him, calmed him down, let him talk and spill out the long litany of beatings and fear. William explained who he was, what faith he followed, and asked if the young man was a Christian. He nodded. 'Can we pray together to the same God we both believe in? We can pray for His understanding and His mercy.' He nodded again.

The whole corridor was hushed, listening. The pair spoke quietly with the door shut, but the place bristled with attentive eavesdroppers. Practically every man on this floor envied that lad his wise counsellor. No one had ever talked to them so gently or bothered to listen so well.

Father William had a new vocation. He was in demand, Some were time wasters, seeking attention. Others were in genuine need but unsure what words to use. The gaol was quieter most nights, once they knew there was someone to talk to at three in the morning. Harry was amazed how the atmosphere changed. There was less jeering at the nightmare screamers. Brutes and bullies newly arrived would be tamed by the sound of an old man comforting a distressed inmate. Jim heard some of them softly weeping.

This went on for months. It was worse in the long dark nights as the year descended into winter. Enclosed in their shadow-filled unheated cells, prisoners had more time to dwell on the where their lives had taken a wrong direction, or had been forced into bad choices.

1692

QUARANTINE

Out of the depths I cry to you, O Lord,
Lord, hear my voice!
My soul is waiting for the Lord,
I count on his word.
My soul is longing for the Lord
more than a watchman for daybreak.

(Ps. 129)

Winter was always a difficult time. Offenders are rarely the
heatlthiest of the populace. They succumbed to whatever
struck down the rest of the town, but had no loving wives to
tend to them. The surgery, a rudimentary treatment room,
was set up to deal with major incidents like amputations,
firearms wounds, stitching up gashes after brawls, lancing
boils. Usually a master-barber would deal with these when
summoned. A physician rarely was required.

Becca had been scrupulous in keeping William
supplied with fresh linen and soap balls so he could
keep himself clean. She regularly changed the stuffing in
his mattress and boil-washed the linen cover. This had
kept William safe and in good health for the first years

of his time in Leicester gaol. In these newer premises Becca continued this regime, convinced she was doing her utmost. Father William had significantly changed his routine, however. He no longer kept apart from the rougher ranks. In the small hours of the morning he was escorted to their cells to console them, and with no other option, would naturally sit beside them on their pallet while he let them unravel their woes. This charitable act exposed him to their lice and fleas.

At first he accepted the ache in his joints as the price of his eighty-three years. He had, by and large, got off lightly. Becca noticed he was coughing more. He said he always had a cold as the seasons changed, surely she remembered. October was beatuiful in the countryside, with the full palette of colours in the foliage, but in prison it only meant sharp chilly nights and shorter afternoons. It hurt to read. His eyes must be weakening even more; the briefest spell with his Office seemed to bring on a headache. Becca felt their was a definite deterioration in his general condition, but what could she expect? He wasn't going to live forever. She'd have liked to keep a closer watch on him, but her leg simply would not heal.

She'd had that stupid fall, just a careless trip off the back steps in the kitchen after a summer shower, the worn steps still slippery. Months ago. Something isn't right. The ankle doesn't sit like it should, stays swollen and discoloured. After preparing the big luncheon she finds the leg is throbbing fiercely and she's about useless. Usually, on Tuesday and Friday afternoons she and Tom would set off in the cart to sort out William's supplies of fresh laundry and a few home-cooked treats. This last month Becca has been managing to maintain his support, but has had to send Tom on his own to deliver the basket. The woman couldn't cope with climbing into the cart, a juddering ride, and more time spent hobbling into the prison. Each morning her every thought is just to survive until the lunch business is finished so she can prop up her leg and rest. John keeps telling her it's a sign: she must stop waiting hand and foot on these folks and let him provide for them both.

For the past two weeks, Tom has not been allowed to enter the prison. No visitors are permitted by order. Tom hands in his basket and waits; the guard on the door drops off the contents in William's cell and returns the basket to Tom filled with the next load for washing. When he asks if William is well, the guard simply nods and shoos him away. The first week he was told why.

There is an outbreak of fever inside and the corporation is terrified it will spread to the general populace. The physician diagnosed one of the upstairs inmates with gaol fever. No one took any notice of his condition at first. He seemed to have the same hacking cough and foul mood as everyone else trying to make the best of a hard life. The fever alternating with chills had Toby sending for help. Five days later the tell-tale rash appeared on the man's chest, then began to spread. Anyone who'd had any contact with him was in serious danger.

Father William had spent a night or two with the stricken man. Toby said it would be best if he curtailed his chats with any other prisoners, just until the crisis had passed. They both left unsaid the fact that the priest may have already been infected. It could take up to two weeks to develop the physician had explained, so the crisis would not end when this lone man breathed his last. A fit, well-nourished man in his prime had a chance of survival, but the poor wretches who ended up in the cells had little reason to hope.

The man was burning up, muttering, calling for loved ones. There were moments of lucidity. Toby and Jimmy masked their faces, believing the sickness was carried in the air. They brought him pitchers of ale, bowls of broth to slake his thirst, but didn't linger by his side. The man knew he was dying. He called for the priest. Toby told him he'd seen him often enough, it wasn't fair to risk him getting ill too. The man grew desperate, shouting. The whole building could hear him.

William met Toby at the bottom of the stairs, 'I'll go to him, if you help me up.'

'You know what this means? I can't protect you.'

William nodded slowly. 'What am I if I refuse to see a dying man? If this is the Lord's will, then so be it. If the last act I'm capable of is to help this man prepare to meet his God, then I shall accept that as a grace that has been granted me.'

It did not come as a surprise when the fever overcame him. He'd half known he was ailing for days, and had kept to his cell. Toby could hardly bear to look in on him. He felt responsible, for offering him the chance he knew the cleric could not, would not refuse, to ease the suffering of those filthy murderers, drunks and rogues. William's judge said he was to be treated well and kept apart from that rough sort. A wise man. William would still be hale and hearty if I'd obeyed that ruling, he kept telling himself.

William grabbed Toby's wrist as the gaoler set down a fresh pitcher by his bed. 'Thank you. Don't look so distressed, Toby. I knew this was coming. I'm not afraid.'

'I'm so sorry, William, it's all my fault. Please, please forgive me.'

'Nothing to forgive. You care for those men and sought help for them, that is no sin. I chose to do what I could. It was my free choice, not your fault. Do not ever think that.'

Toby sighed and could not reply. William squeezed his hand and begged a favour.

'Whatever, whatever you want, if it's in my power, I'll do it.'

'In a few more days I'll be past asking, so I'm begging you now. When I'm in my last hour will you read some psalms over me? It's hard to face the end without the Last Rites. Maybe I will hear you, I hope so. ..

'I know fever victims must be buried quickly. Try and get a message up to Belgrave. Father Gervase will say a Mass for me...let the Society know.' It was an enormous effort to concentrate. He closed his eyes to summon the energy, 'Tell Becca it wasn't frightening, you looked after me. Thank her, thank her...bless her...bless you.' He drifted off, exhausted.

Toby watched and waited. He searched his King James Bible to see which psalms he should read. Some verses taunted him, tested his faith like Psalm 90: *I will say of the Lord, He is my refuge and my fortress: my God; in him will I trust. /Surely he shall deliver thee from the snare of the fowler, and from the noisome pestilence.* No, this good man of faith was not delivered from the pestilence.

Psalm 120 was better:The Lord is your guard and your shade; at your right side he stands.By day the sun shall not smite you nor the moon in the night. The Lord will guard you from evil, he will guard your soul. The Lord will guard your going and coming both now and forever. Toby felt he was finding words that William would expect to hear. He hoped he could hear him. Out of the depths have I cried unto thee, O Lord./Lord, hear my voice… If thou, Lord, shouldest mark iniquities, O Lord, who shall stand?/ I wait for the Lord, my soul doth wait, and in his word do I hope. (Ps.129/130) He remembered his mother had a favourite, the 23rd psalm, The Lord is my shepherd…that felt right. Toby stopped on the last lines, Surely goodness and mercy shall follow me all the days of my life: and I will dwell in the house of the Lord for ever.

He had a few thoughts of his own to convey on behalf of William Bentney.

1692

NOVEMBER

> *May eternal light shine on him, O Lord,*
> *with all your saints forver, for you are rich in*
> *mercy.*
> *Give him eternal rest, O Lord,*
> *and may perpetual light shine on him for ever,*
> *for you are rich in mercy.*
> *(Communion antiphon, Funeral Mass)*

Becca returned to the gaol the day after her visit to the convicts' graveyard. This time she was accompanied by both Tom and her husband John. She wanted answers. Tom was very quiet, uncomfortable as she worked herself up, complaining to John about how she had been left in the dark about Father William's condition. He was beginning to feel just as aggrieved on her behalf. He shot a stern look across to his brother.

Tom was worried she'd create a scene at the door, and Harry would put her straight in his usual very few words. It would all rebound on Tom. It was better if he spoke up before things got out of hand. 'It's not their fault, Becca. I knew, I knew something was wrong, but didn't tell you.'

Becca couldn't believe what she hearing, 'You knew? What did you know? When? Why couldn't you tell me?'

Tom took a deep breath and tried to make his choices sound reasonable, although he'd been regretting them ever since, 'Toby answered the door a few weeks ago. His face was masked. There was an outbreak of fever and no visitors were allowed. I just dropped off the basket.'

'You said nothing! Was William ill even then?'

'Toby said William was his usual self. Everyone seemed to be coming down with colds but the physician had only seen one man who had the fever. They had to be careful because it spread so easily once it took hold in a place...he said not to worry, William was being kept well apart.'

'So you chose not to worry, and not to worry me, is that it?'

'Of course I worried, but what good would it serve to worry you? I had to trust Toby and Harry and all had it under control as best they could, didn't I?'

'Did you know about this fever, John? Surely Tom couldn't keep this to himself, he must have confided in you? You two are always down the ale-house.' Becca's sense that even her husband was keeping secrets from her had her fix him in her gaze and demand a straight answer.

It was John's turn to be uncomfortable. 'Yes, eventually, not right away, he came out with it, just before he was due to return to the gaol for his second visit that week. He was afraid of what he might hear.'

'And you too thought it best I was not told? What else haven't you told me?'

'There was nothing to tell, we agreed. Not yet. There had been trouble in the past, and nothing had come of it. There was no reason to suspect this time would be any different. Toby said William was well away from the outbreak. You've not been well yourself, and coping with the Hall has so worn you out, I couldn't lay more on you. If there was any solid news, you know you'd have been the first to be told.'

'So what happened this week? You returned with a basket of washing on Tuesday, did no one say he was ill?'

'Harry answered the door, took the delivery, said nothing and brought back the soiled things. Very keen to see the back of me. He slammed the door in my face as I was trying to ask. I couldn't tell what was going through his mind because he was wearing that mask. In the end I thought he'd probably had a rough night. If anything was wrong with William, most likely he would have said. At least I thought he would've.'

'Right, and so on Friday, he had no need of anything from us, and you came back to tell me our priest had died. So you brought me to the criminals' graveyard Saturday. Is that everything we know?' The two men nodded. 'Then let's see what else the guards can tell us.'

Toby answered the door, muffled in his mask. He'd been expecting them. He explained more with hand signals than words that they'd not be allowed in, but to go down the side alley to the back yard. They waited at the back gate and he came round to let them in, ushering them over to Moll's bench. He grabbed a small keg for a stool.

The questions came thick and fast. Toby did his best to explain how gaol fever progressed, how until the actual fever developed it might have felt just like an ordinary cold. The sweats, the chills, the rash made it obvious. At eighty-three he didn't stand a chance. The fever made short work of the old priest. The rash soon appeared; there was no need for a physician. There was nothing he could have done. The end came with a stupor, leading to a a short frantic delirium, then the release into death.

They asked how he might have caught it since he was on a different floor from the other prisoners. This was the question Toby was hoping they wouldn't ask. 'Father William asked to go to comfort the dying, to listen to men who couldn't escape the nightmares that haunted them, to pray with them in the middle of the night if it brought them peace. That's how he came in contact with the fever, by being a priest to his flock.' Toby had not been able to look them in the eye when he told them, he spoke to the ground, staring at his hands.

Becca was sharp. She knew the layout, 'He couldn't get up to them without help. You brought him upstairs, didn't you? Whose idea was it to put him in harm's way? Is that how you looked after a helpless old man?'

Toby met her fierce accusatios, 'Yes, we helped him upstairs when he wished, and yes, I talked over the idea of helping calm the pitiful cries in the middle of the night. He was awake most nights at that hour, long before the noise began. That's why he nodded off during the day. We talked about the dangers, he wasn't sure. Then he prayed about it and decided it was his duty to try. 'If I'm meant to do this, then I'll be given the grace to get on with it.'

'But you told Tom he was well away from the fever victim.'

'Once we knew there was fever, he was kept apart, downstairs. Given how things went, he was probably already ill by then but didn't know it. He offered to pray with a dying fever patient, and we told him not to go, but maybe he did already suspect his time was limited. He worsened soon after. He asked me to read some psalms to him because there'd be no priest to come for him. He taught me to read, you know?'

'Me too,' whispered Becca.

'How was it at the end?'

' He said to tell you it wasn't frightening. Once the fever had drained all his energy he drifted into a sort of trance. He was halfway on his journey, having left all sense of us behind. It overtook him like a wave swallowing up a ship in a storm. He was there and then he wasn't. I reached out to hold his hand as his breath grew shallow. His nose seemer sharper. His chest stopped. I held his hand to my cheek until the warmth drained away.

'I've seen a lot of death in this job. It's no stranger to a prison. Part of the business, dealing with bodies, binding them up, wrapping the corpse, hefting them onto the cart for burial up the way.

'When there's pestilence, it needs swift work to keep the living free of it. I should have bundled William up as soon as the glass showed no sign of breath, but I couldn't.

'I didn't know how to pray the way he wanted, what he needed, but I couldn't let him go.'

'What happened? He was buried quickly after all..'

'Harry, of course. He found me. The thing with Harry is he's gruffest when he's upset. He stared in at me holding William's hand and the priest clearly dead. He knew he was going to go soon, and knew it would upset me. We'd never had a fellow stay so long with us before, or be so decent. He shouldn't have been locked up. Most men would've spent years shouting down the courts, the judge, everyone for the injustice of it all. He just accepted it, grateful he wasn't hanged. He changed us.

'Course Harry couldn't admit that. His response was typical: he barked at me to get on with the binding. He couldn't stop here another night. 'Rules is rules if you want to see your tomorrows,' he snaps.'

' I have his things ready for you to collect, all except his rosary. When I laid him out I wrapped them round his hands. There had to be some way to set him apart.'

Tom looked up, 'That rosary was the one I made him from dried holly berries from our garden. He said it was full of good memories.'

'And it was you who put the cross over his grave,' Becca added.

'It wasn't much. It won't last. His resting place will soon be forgotten, but I shan't forget.'

Father William's few possessions were stored at Belgrave Hall. His books joined the library of religious texts that its various departed priests had left behind. His walking stick merged with the collection stored in a great Chinese vase by the front door; his reading glass was returned to Lady Compton. Becca asked Master Charles what she should do with his fiddle. 'Where do you think he'd like it to go?' he replied.

'To The Angel I reckon, it seems only right.'

'My thought exactly. You and John must drop in next Friday. That's the night the musicians gather, if I remember rightly, when William used to join them. They can make it sing in his honour. But what for yourself, Becca? After all the years you've known and cared for him, you of all people should have something to remember him by.'

'Well, sir, I took the liberty of keeping his tortoise shell comb, that I used to trim his hair with sometimes. There is something I would like, if you think it wouldn't be too bold.'

'Name it. I can't think of anyone else who has a greater claim to his goods.'

'I found two volumes of poetry amongst his books. Since he taught me to read, it would give me a way to be close to him, to spend time with the words he treasured. Is that asking too much?'

'I think he'd be delighted for you to cherish them. By the way, I noticed his walking stick has been placed with the others in the hall stand.'

'Yes, sir. Mistress Anne had it made for him when he was first arrested.'

'Quite so, I recall her telling me, wondering if he'd be allowed it. I don't imagine she'd be displeased if you made use of it, at least until that leg of yours heals. I'm sure it's what she would have wished.'

'It's a bit grand for the likes of me, sir, but it would be a great help I'm sure. I'll take great care of it, thank you, I'm most grateful.'

Father Gervase said the funeral Mass on Sunday. The garret was packed. Becca set out a table of cold meats, cheese and Master Charles supplied plenty of ale so everyone could toast Father William's memory and recall old times with the gardener priest. Father Gervase and Tom slipped away from the reception. It was quiet in Leicester on a Sunday. No one noticed the simple cart trundling up to the edge of the old boundaries, pulling up by the picket fence. Gervase stepped over to William's plot and said a few quiet prayers, then sprinkled the ground with holy water. Tom stood awkwardly beside him, then made the sign of the cross himself, not sure exactly what he was supposed to do.

He made up his mind to make one more holly berry rosary, for himself.

> *O precious in the eyes of the Lord*
> *is the death of his faithful*
> *Your servant, Lord, your servant am I;*
> *you have loosened my bonds.*
> > *(Mass for the Dead,*
> > *Responsorial Psalm, Ps 114:15-16)*

AFTERWORD

In Plain Sight is a fictional account of the life of Father William Bentney based on historical facts. Various characters have had to be invented to construct a narrative and fill in gaps from the scant clues in his known biography.

William Bentney was a native of Cheshire and born in 1609. There is no information about his family, so I credited him as coming from a well-to-do farming background, as Cheshire was famed for its agriculture at that period. It would explain his known ease with manual labourers, as well as more educated members of society. He entered the Society of Jesus on September 7, 1630 and was sent out to the English Mission in 1640. His first posting was to the Hampshire District, but in 1652 he was transferred to the Derbyshire district (designated the College of the Immaculate Conception), which included Leicester.

The Byerleys owned the manor house, Belgrave Hall in the village of Belgrave, just outside Leicester's town limits. They were known Catholics and had regularly housed priests to serve the local area. William Byerley was a wool merchant with warehouses in the town. Before the Civil War the family had lived in the town, but as conditions in the town became more crowded and the buildings in dire need of repair, William moved out to Belgrave, to the largest house in the village, purchased from the Hastings family. They were fortunate to escape before war broke out because the town fabric was badly damaged during the fighting. In Belgrave they found fresher air and room for a garden. William's first wife, Jane Matthew, died, as did their young son. Elizabeth Claxton, his second wife, gave birth to a second son, Charles, and a daughter, Anne.

Wishing a decent tutor for his children as well as a chaplain, William petitioned the Jesuits to supply one. William Bentney was not able to take up his post until 1652, after the war. Information in the Leicester Records Office includes a fine description of the old Hall and its gardens at the time William Bentney would have been there. Since many hidden priests were nominally described as 'gardeners', I had William help design the Byerley's grounds with a nod to recusant symbolism known to be used as a testament to their faith and an aid to contemplation. Lyveden, the family home of the Treshams, provided this background. The garden plans were drawn up by the Tresham's steward, George Levens.

The original Belgrave manor house stayed in the possession of the Byerleys and their descendents, the Beaumonts, until about 1830. They owned it, but did not always reside there. The present Georgian building was built in 1709-13 for Edmund Craddock. The turnpike, mentioned in the text in a recorded recollection of the Byerley's garden, was not built until 1726. By then the new inhabitant, a Mr. Nixon, said to be 'a respectable grazier', had dug up the fine garden and had substituted 'turnips &c.' which the history comments 'many persons may judge more useful'.

The records also detailed who lived in the various cottages, information which helped to populate the narrative. Local history volumes describe the usual festivities, including children going from door to door seeking Valentine Buns, hiring practices, and minstrels playing for Christmas celebrations and for civic guests. Catholic histories note the secrecy with which members of the congregation gathered to hear Mass. When the present Belgrave Hall was built some remains of the old manor-house were transferred to the Belgrave Constitutional Club on Loughborough Road. It was said that the window from the Catholic chapel could be seen on the north side of the building. Currently, the building at 201 Loughborough Road is owned by the Sri Jeya Durga Temple, which seems a fitting testimony to the diversity that has always characterised Leicester. Enquiries about the chapel window have been fruitless. The outer fabric of the building would benefit from serious investment to repair and maintain it. It is highly doubtful the chapel window has survived.

The Angel Inn was a famous watering hole in Leicester, marked on a Plan of Medieval Leicester as being on the east side of the Saturday marketplace, within the old town walls, not far from East Gate. It's a bit far from Belgrave Hall for a it to be Ben and William's 'local', but it served the narrative purpose of giving the priest a way of being known to the wider townsfolk, so that when he was later accused, and evidence against him was sought, those people who knew the man refused to testify, even if offered inducements.

William Byerley's children continued to maintain Bentney after their father died in 1653. Charles married Mary Cuttler. They had three children, another Charles, Joseph and a daughter, Elizabeth, named after her grandmother. The family tree in the *History and Antiquities of Leicestershire* records sadly that this toddler and her grandmother both died on March 4, 1661.

Anne Byerley married Humphrey Wharton of London. There were no further details about her life. The narrative has her returning to Belgrave as a widowed second wife who is not well treated by her husband's children by his first marriage. Anne was a useful vehicle to explore the rights of widows, their relative freedom, the education of women and the general move to extend literacy to the working class. Antonia Fraser's volumes, *The Weaker Vessel,* gave clear examples from this period. In writing a biography of a man who outlived most of the significant characters in his life, Anne also provided a lynchpin between generations.

There are countless historical books written about the Titus Oates' revelations of a supposed Popish plot. The main furor occured in the years 1678-80, but William Bentney was not arrested until two years later. He was not implicated in Oates' list of traitors, but he was a known Jesuit. Local Catholic history suggested that a brother in the Byerley house betrayed the priest, in conjunction with Sir Henry Beaumont. In the Byerley family at that time Joseph was a likely choice for the betrayer; he died at the age of twenty-two, old enough to have taken umbridge with the cleric. I fabricated a reason, and found a way to steer him towards the local MP, Sir Henry Beaumont. There seemed no need to be melodramatic and have the lad commit suicide, or meet with violence. A drunken riding accident sufficed. Shipping a wayward son to the colonies was a reasonable option the fictional couple considered before the tragedy. If Joseph had emigrated, there would have been great oppurtunities to succeed in Rhode Island.

The Beaumont family had both Catholic and Church of England members. The Catholic Beaumonts were out at Gracedieu, near Thringstone, Leicestershire, Sir Thomas and his five lovely daughters (one of whom married Charles Byerley the younger). In more recent times it was the home of the De Lisle family. Grace Dieu Manor is now a Catholic school. Sir Henry Beaumont was based at Stoughton Grange, a country house in the parish of Stoughton, Leicestershire. He was MP for the area from 1679-1685. An observer at the treason trial mentioned a Justice Gilbert as being particularly keen to see any Jesuit treated harshly. There was no such Justice in Leicestershire. It was in a local history of Derbyshire, *The West Hallam Heritage* by B. J. Parker, that a George Gilbert appeared. He did serve as a justice and was the owner of Locko, an estate in the parish of Lullington. He was a neighbour to the Powtrell family of West Hallam, who were known to be Catholics.

Gilbert had been spying on his neighbours for years. He secured a warrant to search the Powtrell's when the Oates frenzy was raging, but the Jesuit district superior, George Busby, had fled to the continent. Anne Powtrell, the wife of the owner, was Busby's niece. He'd been the Powtrell's chaplain for six or seven years. Gilbert waited and watched. The priest returned when he thought the fuss was over and was spotted in the gardens. Gilbert brought searchers twice to the house and eventually found him. Parker gives a detailed account of Gilbert's efforts and the trick he used to make the Powtrells think his search had ended unsuccessfully. Busby was found in the roof space and sent for trial in Derby, staying at his lawyer's house to await the Assizes court which dealt with treason cases and only met twice a year. It was common for those accused who had financial backing and were more refined to stay in the more comfortable lodging of their lawyer rather than in gaol.

It was while he was in custody that Joseph Byerley's tip-off alerted Sir Henry Beaumont to the strong possibility that Busby and Bentney could both be tried. Jesuit records of the College of the Immaculate Conception, the Derbyshire District, contain details of William Bentney's trial taken from an observer's letter found in the Public Records Office, Brussels. Gilbert used the same witnesses from the Powtrell's former employees to testify against Bentney as he had used against Busby. He was found guilty, condemned to death, but the judge was uneasy about the harsh verdict.

He promised to go to London and have it respited, which he did. Bentney asked , 'as he was of broken health and decayed in years, that he might not not be detruded into the common prison, among the common malefactors.' The judge agreed, 'seeing that he was an aged gentleman, he should be well treated, and have the privilege of a better prison.'

Once in custody, it would have been up to his benefactors, the Byerleys, to provide for his upkeep. Charles senior would have delegated this to his staff. With the scandal of his son's betrayal of their chaplain, followed by Joseph's sudden death, the family would have kept a low profile. The fact that William Bentney lived another ten years after his trial when he claimed to be in 'broken health', shows that he must have been well treated, which the fictional version tries to convey. In letters to the Jesuit Father General, there is mentioned the great difficulty of finding means to support the members of the Province, who were either lying in prisons or had no patrons to whom to resort. Many of the noblemen and gentry who formerly retained a chaplain were then afraid or unable to do so, both on account of their reduced means(from fines) and because of the dangerous times. It is to the Byerley's credit that they did maintain their support regardless.

Charles Byerley senior died in 1682, the year of Bentney's first arrest and trial. His surviving son, also called Charles, succeeded him as master of Belgrave. Charles the younger married Jane Beaumont of the Grace Dieu Beaumonts. This couple outlived Father Bentney, both dying in 1738.

The unexpected release from prison prompted by James II's accession to the throne did not give Bentney any peace of mind. The political situation was very volatile. Resentment and suspicion of James were increasing. His forceful, threatening approach and Catholic agenda as his reign progressed stoked fears of a nation being forced back to the Old Faith. Fears were only increased when his wife produced a son and heir. Bentney would have expected to be hunted down once more as James' opponents had always insisted that James had exceeded his powers by releasing him.

Jesuit records state that Bentney left the district (the College of the Immaculate Conception) and sought a place of safety in the St. George's district. This includes Worcestershire. Several well-known homes in this area contained priest-holes. When William was re-arrested in 1689 he was found in a priest-hole, but no mention is made of the actual house. I chose Hindlip House because of its history and association with Nicholas Owen, the Jesuit priest-hole designer. Placing Bentney in a house that had been searched after the Gunpowder Plot, over eighty years earlier, was more dramatic. It was also the site from which Owen himself was captured. Tony Reynolds in, *St. Nicholas Owen, Priest-Hole Maker(Gracewing, 2014)*, gives quite detailed information on the type of hides Owen constructed and how those concealed were sustained whilst in hiding.

The site of Hindlip House is now the area police headquarters, but a nearby period property, also associated with Owen, Harvington Hall, is open to the public. It was the hides in this house that were used as a reference. It displayed testimony from priests who had eluded capture as to the conditions while in hiding, and how they survived. It was useful to see the confines of these spaces rather than only read about them.

The owner of Hindlip at the time of the Gunpowder Plot was Thomas Habington.His wife was the sister-in-law of Lord Mounteagle, whose letter revealed the plot. Habington's son, William, was a minor poet. The house was eventually left to Sir William Compton. His grandson, also William Compton, married Catherine Bond and was created a baronet by James II. He died in 1698. The Worcestershire county council archivist claims the Compton family were not known to be recusants, but could not say with certainty that they were not. If the head of the household swore the Act of Allegiance and attended Church of England services a few times a year, the rest of the family could escape notice. The text implies that only Lady Compton was a serious Catholic, but if the family was favoured by James, perhaps there were Catholic leanings in reality.

Harvington Hall has a hide for vestments beneath a couple of floorboards in the garret chapel. The narrative transfers this feature to Bentney's room. Harvington also has a priest hole hidden in the main staircase concealed behind a jewel safe, which is where the text has Bentney being hidden and eventually found. Also on display was a set of rosary beads made from dried holly berries, strung on twine with a simple wooden cross. It seemed apt that a man ostensibly a gardener should carry such a humble, home-made set. My grandfather carried a similar hand made set, knotted twine with a flimsy wooden cross. His were darkened with oil and sweat from spending his World War I service in the belly of a wooden mine sweeper, stoking the furnace. Powerful images, these simple mementoes.

William Bentney was eighty when he was found in a priest-hole. He could not have managed without help, strong physical assistance. He needed a manservant. He also needed to have someone to talk to, and would not be able to be as openly familiar with the Comptons as he had been with the Byerleys, given the need to keep his presence known to as few as possible. The British involvement in Barbados began in 1625, initially to produce tobacco. Irish indentured labourers were not productive in the stifling heat and the crop was not as good as the Virginia varieties. By the 1640s sugar and slaves were the answer to the island's prosperity. The gentry in Barbados were the richest men in British America. George Fox had visited the island, preaching that 'all blacks, whites and tawnies' were equally God's creatures. There were some who, like Richard Baxter in 1673, thought it a crime to 'equal men to beasts.' It was common for house slaves to accompany their masters back to England. In the narrative, the son has completed his education in England. His manservant, Thomas, studied to assist his young master to succeed. It was possible to purchase one's freedom. This was the arrangement suggested in the text; Joseph was cleverer than the young man he attended. It became more convenient to let him go and find employment with the Comptons.

There was a suggestion that William Bentney was tried a second time upon his recapture. After an extensive search of *Cobbett's Treason Trials,* which has documented every such trial throughout the period and beyond, there is no record of a second trial. In King William's rush to quell any support for James' Irish invasion by those Jesuits freed by

James II, it would have been much more expedient simply to reinstate the original conviction, having declared James' action illegal.

The old borough gaol was built in 1614 and stood at the corner of High Cross Street and Causeway Lane. It is said to have been 'very close and never whitewashed with very offensive sewers.' In James II's reign in 1685 land was purchased on the east side of High Cross Street for a new gaol. This area had long been used as a gaol site, the first being built in 1309. In present day Leicester on Highcross Street look for the shop dated '1712' in the brickwork. To the left of the shop, between it and the next red brick building are the remains of another, stone building. This is the only surviving remnant, stone work from the old borough gaol.

It is not certain whether this location does date back to the gaol that William Bentney spent his last years in. The wall seems likely to be part of a later prison, built in 1790, one that Leicester's gigantic Daniel Lambert once presided over. Daniel followed his father into the prison service. His father had been in charge of a bridewell (prison for minor offenders) also on Highcross Street. Prisons on this street changed their remit from being borough prisons or county prisons when one might fall into disrepair, or another was built, and the records are inexact as to specific location along this street, except that it was on the east side. The Records Office does hold a 1685 plan of the new gaol which provided a reference point for the fictional text. The architect's noted that the outer walls were to be one and a half bricks in thickness, (not the stonework seen in the remnant). Lambert's prison was said to have been built on the site of a previous prison. It's possible but there is no certainty that this was the actual site.

Gaol fever is what killed William Bentney. It is typhus, spread through bites from lice and fleas, and common in crowded, unhygenic surroundings. Amongst those with poor nutrition and little resistance, it can claim up to sixty per cent of its victims. The incubation period lasts between one and two weeks. It causes a headache and cough which might initially be thought to be a common cold. The illness progresses to fever, severe muscle pain, chills and a sensitivity to light. A tell-tale rash of red spots on on the chest appears five days after the fever, and the spots gradually spread to the extremities. The victim descends into a stupor leading to delirium, then death. As hearing is the last sense to fade, the narrative has Toby reading to William as he sank deeper into his semi-conscious state. Father Bentney was the last English Jesuit to suffer in the persecutions.

In searching for possible names for warders in the *Records of the Borough of Leicester, Vol. VI,* I came across a John Norrice who was on the constables' staff in 1688. He became the burly gaoler who gave William fireman's lifts to the upper floor.

The criminals' burial ground occupied the present site of Infirmary Square in Leicester. In 1998 a Blue Plaque was erected on the wall of the maternity wing of the Leicester Royal Infirmary which faces the Square to honour the memory of William Bentney and pays tribute to the people of Leicester who refused to condemn him. It was unveiled by the then provincial of the Jesuits, the Very Rev. James Crampsey SJ.

The present Provincial of the British Jesuits, Fr Dermot Preston SJ, accepts that Father Bentney is 'something of a forgotten hero', but that the Society 'regard Fr. William Bentney SJ with great affection and he has not been ignored.' He explained that he is not considered 'venerable' because 'this is a technical status that the official Church decides on.' He explained:

> It would seem from documents in Rome that a pragmatic decision was taken before 1970 to generally only canonize those who died in public... The British Jesuits still has an impressive list of nineteen 'Blesseds' who will probably never be canonised. There are lots of accounts of Catholics, not just Jesuits, who died for their faith but were not put forward for canonisation- the 40 English and Welsh Martyrs were a cross-section of lay people, priests and religious, adding to St. Thomas More and St. John Fisher who were processed earlier in the 20th century.

Father Preston is 'sure that Father Bentney...is actually rubbing shoulders with the formally proclaimed martyrs.' Their roles of 'giving witness to later generations indicates that each continues to do so: some, like Edmund Campion are very high profile, but others like Bentney in Leicester... inspire others on a smaller, more intimate, scale. Their role is no less, just different.'

Hindlip Hall

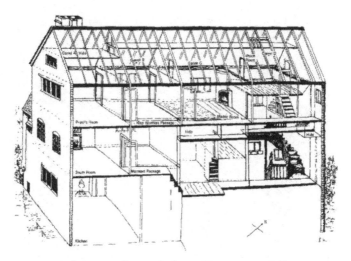

A diagram of priest hides in Harvington Hall

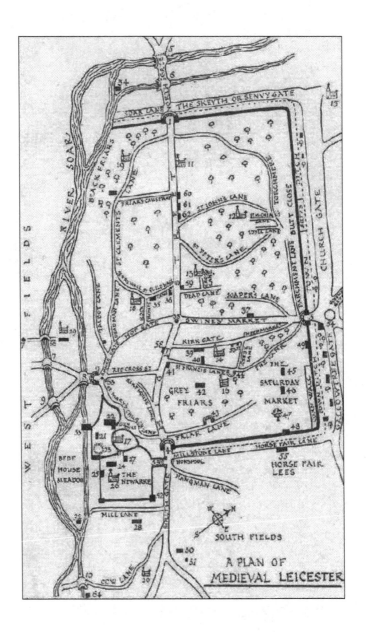

A PLAN OF
MEDIEVAL LEICESTER

KEY TO THE PLAN OF MEDIEVAL LEICESTER

1. North Gate
2. West Gate
3. East Gate
4. South Gate
5. North Bridge
6. Frogmire Bridge
7. Bow Bridge
8. West Bridge
9. Braunston Bridge
10. Cow Bridge
11. All Saint's Church
12. St. Michael's Church
13. St. Peter's Church
14. St. Martin's Church
15. St. Margaret's Church
16. Grey Friars' Church
17. St. Mary's Church
18. St. Nicholas' Church
19. St. Clement's Church
20. St. Sepulchre's Church
21. Castle Hall
22. Castle House
23. Castle Mound
24. Newarke Hospital
33. Castle Gate
34. North Mill
35. Old Mayor's Hall
36. Blue Boar Inn
37. Lord's Place
38. High Cross
39. Guildhall
40. Wyggeston's Hospital
41. Henry Costeyn's House
42. The Grey Friars' Priory
43. Grey Friars' Gateway
44. Grey Friars' Gateway
45. Shambles and Draperie
46. The Gainsborough
47. Elm Tree
48. Green Dragon Inn
49. Angel Inn
50. Maiden Head Inn
51. St. George's Guildhall
52. Rupert's Tower
53. Newarke Main Gateway
54. Bere Hill
55. Old Barn
56. Little Bow Bridge

25. Dean of Newarke's House

26. Newarke College Church

27. Wyggeston's Chantry House

28. Newarke Grange

29. The Austin Friars

30. Hermitage

31. St. Sepulchre's Well

32. Newarke Mill

57. St. Austin's Well

58. Roger Wygston's House

59. Free Grammar School

60. Shirehall

61. Prisona Regis

62. St. John's Hospital

63. Red Cross

64. Mary Mill

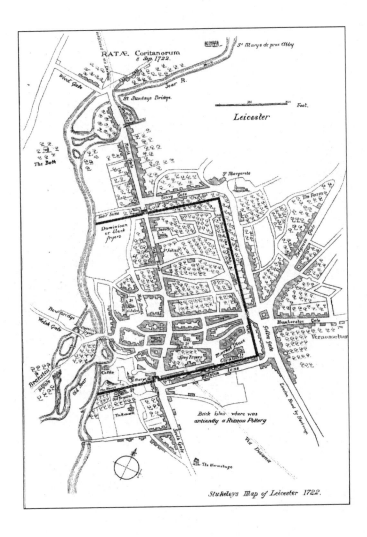

RATÆ. Coritanorum
8 Sep. 1722.

St Marys de pres Abbey

Soar R.

Wood Gate

St Sundays Bridge.

Feet.

Leicester

The Bath

St Margarets

The Farm

Senvy Gate

Soar Lane

Soar Lane

Dominican
or black
fryars

All Saints

St Johns

Sanvey Gate

Humberston Gate

Bowbridge

Welsh Gate

St Nicholas

Humberston Gate

Vernometum

Brehston

Asfoak

Old Port

Castle

St Marys

Grey Fryers

Market Place
Coritani

Soder Gate

London Road by Harborogh

Mouton Lane

The Newark

Brick kilns where was
antiently a Roman Pottery

Soar Gate

Via Devana

The Hermitage

Stukeleys Map of Leicester 1722.

209